Bonnets and Bugles Series · 3

THE SECRET OF RICHMOND MANOR

GILBERT MORRIS

MOODY PRESS
CHICAGO

Scripture quotations are taken from the King James Version of the
Bible.

ISBN: 0-8024-0913-X

3 5 7 9 10 8 6 4 2

Printed in the United States of America

To Andrea Smith,
my blonde, blue-eyed Texan granddaughter,
with all my affection.
I know you'll grow up to be perfect in every way
—exactly like your mother!

Contents

1

Who'd Eat an Old Frog?

Leah Carter bent over the wood cookstove and opened the oven door. A delicious aroma wafted out. She inhaled it with enjoyment, then pulled out the large pan and placed it on the table. Looking around, she found the broom in the corner and quickly removed one of the straws. Coming back to the table, she leaned over the cake that bulged over the pan and plunged the straw into the top.

"Just right!" she said with satisfaction. She placed the cake aside and then stepped back to the stove, where a saucepan of chocolate was bubbling. She stood watching it for awhile, and when it looked right she picked up the pan and went to the cake. Carefully she added the icing and then, putting the saucepan down, examined her creation. "You look like a fine cake," she said.

"You talking to yourself, Leah?"

She jumped, startled, and turned to the man who had come in. "Uncle Silas," she scolded, "I wish you wouldn't sneak up on me like that!"

"I wasn't sneaking." Silas Carter grinned at her with an air of innocence. He was a small man with a full white beard and a pair of merry blue eyes. "I came clomping in like a herd of elephants." A sly smirk touched his lips, and he said, "I think you must be thinking about some young man."

"I was not!" Leah protested.

"Well, have it your own way." Uncle Silas walked over to the table and looked down at the cake. "How 'bout I have a piece of that?"

"No, that's for supper."

"Well, let me just taste the icing."

When her uncle reached out to draw his finger across the frosting, Leah squealed, "Don't you dare!" Turning, she picked up the saucepan. "Here, you can scrape the pan." She watched him greedily lick the spoon, then begin scraping at the thick icing on the inside. "You're just like a child," she exclaimed, shaking her head.

Silas did not stop eating the icing. "Well, I did without good cooking so long," he said between bites, "I don't miss many chances."

"I hope you've got something to do today," Leah said. "I can't cook with you underfoot all the time."

"I'll just sit right over here." Silas drew a cane-bottomed chair from under the table and moved it against the wall. Carefully he sat down and tilted it back, placing his heels on the rung. "Now this is what I like. Lots of good food and a fine-looking young woman to do the housework! I should have thought of this a long time ago."

"You're spoiled," Leah accused the old man.

Silas nodded cheerfully. "About time, I say." He gave the spoon another healthy swipe with his tongue. "If I had known I could've had a life like this, I would've gotten sick a long time ago."

Silas's two nieces, Leah and Sarah Carter, had come all the way to Virginia from Kentucky to care for him after he had gotten ill. They had, he insisted, saved his life from the awful woman he'd hired to take care of him. He had grown very fond of the

10

girls and had been saddened when Sarah had to return home. She had had a slight misunderstanding with the Confederate authorities. In fact, she'd been falsely accused of being a spy and had been forced to leave Richmond.

Looking over at Leah, Silas said, "I'm sure glad you could stay and take care of me. I miss Sarah, though. She sure is a fine girl!"

Leah was busy rattling pans, getting ready to cook the evening meal. "I miss her too. And Pa and Ma—and Esther."

"Too bad Sarah had to go home. I was sad to see it happen—but not as sorry as Tom."

He gave the spoon one more lick, then gruffly said, "I guess he's all she writes about in her letters." He handed the pan to Leah and said, "What time are the Majors boys coming?"

She began cleaning the saucepan. "They said they'd be here late this afternoon."

"I was surprised that they could get off, what with this battle shaping up," Uncle Silas said.

The mention of the battle caused Leah to frown. "I guess it's only because Lt. Majors is still weak from being in that ole Yankee prison camp. I still don't like the way he looks. He ought to take a month off."

"I don't think he's going to get it, though, the way the Yankees are headed this way. We'll need every man we can get to hold off them blue-bellies." Silas tilted his chair forward and stood to his feet. "What all we having for supper? I'm hungry already."

"You get out of here, Uncle Silas," Leah scolded. "I can't get a thing done with you around, and you're not going to spoil your supper by getting into that cake!"

Silas shook his head sadly. "That was exactly my intention," he said. "But you're the boss in the kitchen, so I'll go out and hoe the beans a little bit."

Leah, looking out the window, smiled as her uncle picked up a hoe and headed for the garden. As he began hoeing slowly and methodically, she thought again how strange it was that she was here in Richmond. She'd grown up in Kentucky, but when the war came that state had split in two—half for the Union and half for the South. The Carter family had been for the Union—her own brother, Royal, was serving in the Union army. The thought of Royal made her sad for a moment. She was afraid he was in the Army of the Potomac that everyone said was headed for Richmond.

She thought of the job of getting the chicken ready for supper. She didn't like that part of cooking—killing the chicken. But it was something that had to be done.

She went out into the chicken yard where the white birds flocked to her, expecting to be fed. *I wish there was some way to eat chickens without killing them*, she thought. She loved animals, and it was hard to choose one, but she did. She quickly went through the ritual of killing the bird and picking the feathers off. When she came back into the house, she complained, "I should've waited and made Jeff do that."

As she cut the chicken into parts and put them in a bowl, she thought about Jeff Majors. He and Tom were the two sons of Lt. Nelson Majors, and Leah had known them all her life. They had been neighbors back in Kentucky. Lt. Majors was from Virginia though, and after Fort Sumter was fired on he'd taken his family South. Here he'd joined the Confederate army, as had his sons, Tom and Jeff.

As Leah thought of Jeff, her eyes brightened. "I wish he didn't have to go to that war. He's not really old enough—only fifteen." Jeff was a drummer boy in his father's company. She and Jeff had grown up together, were more like brother and sister, and he'd said he was glad she'd come to Richmond, for he had been lonesome for her.

Finally all the dinner preparations were completed. Just as she finished, Leah heard her uncle call out, "Here they come, Leah."

She whipped off her apron and ran out the door. She stopped on the porch as three men in a wagon waved and called to her.

Leah looked for Jeff, who sprang out of the wagon first. He was a tall boy with the blackest hair she'd ever seen. His eyes also were black. He was wearing a gray Confederate uniform with buttons down the front and looked very handsome, she thought. She wouldn't say so, however.

As he came up to her, she pouted. "I should have known you'd come in time for supper. You never miss a meal, do you?"

Jeff Majors grinned. "I'd be a fool if I did, with as good a cook as you are."

His dark eyes gleamed with humor, and he looked her over. She was wearing a light blue dress today with white trim around the neck and sleeves and had tied her long blonde hair with a single bow.

13

"Why, you look right pretty, Leah. It's always good when you have a pretty cook instead of an ugly one."

Leah flushed with pleasure, for Jeff didn't pay her many compliments. "You wouldn't care if an *ape* cooked your food, Jeff Majors!" She turned then to greet his father and brother and thought, *I reckon Nelson Majors is one of the handsomest men in the world.*

Lt. Majors was indeed fine looking, over six feet tall, dark-skinned, having the same black hair that Jeff had. He had hazel eyes, however, that were very unusual. He bowed formally to Leah and said, "Miss Leah, I'm sorry for you—a troop of hungry soldiers here to be fed."

Leah took the hand he held out and, when he kissed it, blushed. "All you officers talk fancy," she said.

"So do we corporals." Tom Majors, tall and dark like his father, came to shake Leah's hand himself. He grinned at her. "I feel like I could eat a bear."

"Well, we don't have any bears," she said. "But you sit out here on the porch and talk. Supper'll be ready as soon as I call you."

She went back inside and quickly put the chicken on to fry. As it did, she set the table, putting on Uncle Silas's best white tablecloth. She placed a bowl of fresh flowers, including violets and daisies, in the middle of the table. By the time she'd done all that and mashed the potatoes, the chicken was almost done. She went to the door and called, "Come and get it while it's hot."

The four men came in, and Lt. Majors's eyes opened wide as he looked at the table. "Why, this is like eating at a fancy hotel in Richmond, only better."

Tom said almost reverently as he sniffed the air, "That doesn't smell like anything we get to eat in camp. Come on, let's lay our ears back and pitch into it!"

Jeff laughed. "You've got the manners of a wild hog, Tom."

Tom hit his younger brother on the shoulder. "My manners are as good as yours, I reckon, Brother."

The men sat down and spoke of how pretty the table was set.

When Leah had brought the heaping platter of fried chicken and set it down, she seated herself. "There! We can get started."

Silas bowed his head, and the others followed his example. "Father," he prayed, "we thank You for this food. We thank You for these guests, and we pray for our folks at home. We acknowledge that every good gift comes from You. We pray this in the name of Jesus. Amen."

"Amen!" Lt. Majors said and looked around the loaded table. "Well, we're not going to be hungry if we get on the outside of this food." He looked at the golden fried chicken, the pork chops, the heaping bowl of mashed potatoes, a bowl of poke sallet, and other vegetables. Then he picked up a piece of fresh-baked bread and took a bite. "Oh, my!" He sighed. "I feel like I'm going to commit gluttony."

They all fell to, and Leah was pleased at the way everyone ate. She kept their glasses filled with sweet milk, except for Jeff, who liked buttermilk better. A constant stream of compliments came her way, and she was happy that she'd been able to satisfy them.

When they had slowed down and began shoving their plates back, Leah rose, saying, "You're not through yet."

"Not dessert! I didn't save any room," Jeff protested.

Leah smiled at him sweetly. "That's all right, Jeff. Your father and brother can eat your share."

She left and came back with the cake she had made earlier. When Jeff saw it, he cried out, "Not chocolate-iced cake!"

Leah put down the cake and said innocently, "Too bad you're so full you can't eat any."

"Oh, yeah? Well, you just watch!" He waited as patiently as he could while Leah sliced a piece for each of them.

Jeff started shoveling the dessert into his mouth, and his father said, "Son, you sound like a pig snorting and grunting. I'm ashamed of you."

"I'm sorry, Pa," Jeff said with his mouth stuffed full. "You know how I can resist anything except temptation and dessert."

While the men ate, Leah filled their cups with coffee. "This is about the last of the real coffee," she said. "You'd better enjoy it."

The room became relatively quiet as they ate their dessert. But finally Uncle Silas groaned and said, "Girl, you've done us all in!"

Leah laughed at him, and a dimple popped into her cheek. "It's not my fault you all eat like pigs. You didn't have to."

"Yes, we did, Leah," Tom disagreed. "Any man who wouldn't fill himself up on food like this, why, he's no man at all."

16

They sat around the table then, enjoying one another's company. Soon they began to talk about the war.

Silas asked, "Nelson, what's the talk around headquarters about this army McClelland's got?"

The lieutenant grew serious. He tapped on the white tablecloth with one forefinger and shook his head. "We've got word that he's got over one hundred thousand men."

"How many do we have, Pa?" Jeff asked.

"Well, not that many—maybe seventy thousand in all."

"Well, one rebel could whip five Yankees," Tom said at once.

His father shook his head. "I've heard that said before. But from what I've seen, it's just not so. Those Union soldiers at Bull Run—they fought just about as hard as men could fight."

"But they ran away—we whipped them," Jeff said, chewing on another piece of cake.

Lt. Majors looked at his younger son. "You know, Jeff, in one way I'm sorry we won that battle."

"Sorry we *won!*" Jeff exclaimed. "How can you say that?"

"It's made us overconfident, I'm afraid. All you hear is how we put the run on the Yankees, but one battle's not the war."

Silas nodded. "I think you're right, Nelson. From what I hear, the Yankees went back, put their heads down, and started building a big army and lots of war factories. About all we've done around here is brag about how we whipped them in one battle."

Jeff seemed astounded. "Why, I don't see how

you can talk like that! We've been training and drilling every day. We'll be ready for them."

"I don't doubt we'll do the best we can," his father said, "and after all, we're fighting for our homes, and they're intruders."

They talked for a while longer about the war, then changed the subject. With a battle coming up, they were all a little apprehensive and somewhat depressed. They talked about Esther, Nelson Majors's baby daughter. His wife had died giving birth to Esther, and it had been the Carters, back in Kentucky, who volunteered to take the girl until the Majorses could do better.

"I got a letter from your mother," Lt. Majors said to Leah. He took it out of his pocket. "You might want to read it." He smiled saying, "She claims that Esther's even prettier than you were when you were a baby."

Leah smiled too and took the letter. "Well, she is. She's the prettiest baby I ever saw." As she read, she thought of what a tie Esther had made between the two families. They were divided by the war, but they were together in the task of raising Esther Majors. Handing the letter on to Uncle Silas to read, she said, "I wish I could see her. I miss her so much."

"So do I," the lieutenant said, a frown darkening his face. "A man wants to see his children, and this war won't permit that."

Leah rose and said, "I'll do the dishes."

"Well, I'll help," Tom said. "And you too, Jeff."

"I'm too full," Jeff protested.

But Tom reached down, grabbed him by the hair, and jerked him squealing to his feet.

"You'll help, or I'll strap you." But he laughed.

The young people cleaned up the supper dishes while Silas and Nelson Majors sat on the front porch. The three made a game out of it, laughing and having a good time. Finally they finished and walked out onto the porch too, where they sat until it grew dark.

"Guess we need to go inside. The skeeters are gonna be getting bad," Silas said.

But Jeff said suddenly, "Have you been listening to that big old frog croaking down at the creek?"

"Sounds like a bull, don't he?" Silas nodded. "He's a big one!"

"I'd like to go get me a mess of frogs," Jeff said.

Silas said, "Well, there's a frog gig in the shed over there. It's kind of rusty, but I reckon it'll do. If you want to go, take you a lantern and have at it."

Jeff brightened.

Leah knew he liked any kind of hunting and fishing.

"Come on, Tom," he said. "Let's go."

"Not me. I'm going to go inside and sit down and not do a thing. I've got a feeling we're going to be pretty busy after we go back."

Jeff looked at Leah. "Leah, you come. You can hold the lantern while I do the gigging."

Leah made a face, wrinkling up her nose. "Who'd eat an old frog?"

"I would," Jeff said. He cocked his head to one side and begged, "Come on, Leah. It'll be fun."

"Don't do it, Leah," Tom advised. "He'll have you doing all the work. That's the way Jeff is."

Leah let Jeff coax for a little while, then said, "All right, but I'm going to put on my old clothes." She went to her room and put on a pair of frayed overalls and old shoes.

When she went outside, Jeff was waiting, holding a lantern and a long pole and a sack. "Look! This ought to get 'em." He showed her the gig, which looked like a small pitchfork with four prongs, each having a barb.

Then they walked down to the road, turned, and went on to the creek. The moon had begun to rise—a full moon, like a huge silver dish. By the light of it, Leah could see a small, flat-bottomed wooden boat.

"You get in front," Jeff said. "I'll do the paddling."

Leah scrambled into the boat, holding the lantern carefully.

Jeff got in after her, picked up the paddle, and began to row slowly downstream.

"It's sure quiet," Leah said.

At that moment a huge bull frog said, *"Harumph!"* and she nearly jumped out of the boat.

"Hold it! Hold that lantern up!" Jeff cried.

Leah held the light high, and Jeff brought the boat to a stop. "Let's sit still," he said quietly. He picked up the frog gig and laid down the paddle. "There," he said, "see there—there he is—look at the size of that frog!"

Leah peered into the night, but the lantern light almost blinded her. Finally she did manage to see two gleaming eyes and made out the shape of a large frog perched on the bank.

"Careful now—don't move," Jeff whispered. He picked up the paddle again, maneuvered the boat close to the bank, and grasped the frog gig. Then with a sudden lunge he speared the frog. "Got him!" he exclaimed. He pulled the frog in and removed him from the barbed prongs. As he dropped him into the sack, he said with satisfaction, "Kick all you want to, frog, but you'll be breakfast tomorrow!"

The frog thumped in the sack on the bottom of the boat, and Leah said again, "I don't want to eat any old frog!"

"Did you ever eat frog legs?"

"No, I never did. There's lots of things I haven't eaten."

"Why, you'd like them. They're better than chicken." Jeff nodded. "Come on, let's move on down."

For the next two hours, they paddled slowly down the small stream. Although Leah did not like gigging frogs, she did enjoy being out in the quiet of the night. The mosquitoes, for some reason, were not as bad as usual. They just sang a high, whining song around her ears occasionally. She took a few bites from them, but she was used to that.

Finally Jeff said, "Well, we've got enough for all of us." He turned the boat around, and they made their way back upstream.

"Be careful. Don't fall in the creek," he warned, when Leah got out. He followed her, tied up the boat, and picked up his sack of frogs. "Never got so many big frogs in my whole life." He picked up the gig too. "Let's get back."

They walked up the road by lantern light and moonlight, and when they got back to the house, he said, "Let's go in the backyard—I'll clean these tonight."

Leah went with him, and when they got there she held the lantern for him.

"This won't take long." Jeff pulled a knife from his pocket and opened it.

Leah watched as he cleaned the frogs and admired how efficiently he did it. "I wish I could clean chickens as easy as you do frogs," she said finally.

"Well, frogs don't have feathers." The amber light of the lantern picked up his bright eyes, and he laughed. "That'd be something, wouldn't it—a frog with feathers!"

Soon the frogs were cleaned, and Jeff washed off their catch under the pump. "Pretty good night's work!" he said.

They went inside to find that Tom had gone to bed, but Jeff's father and Uncle Silas were still talking.

Looking up, Silas asked, "Did you get any?"

"Did I get any?" Jeff said. "You never saw such frogs!

"And look how dirty I am!" said Leah. "I'm going to wash up and go to bed. Good night, Jeff."

"Good night, Leah. We'll go again."

As soon as she was gone, the lieutenant grinned at his son. "She's not only pretty, she's a good helper, isn't she? Not every young woman would go frogging with a fellow. You'd better hang onto her."

Jeff said, "Pa, I wish this war was over and we were back in Kentucky."

Nelson Majors's face grew sober. "I wish it too. But you can never go back and be what you were." He looked over at his son, rose, and slapped him on the shoulder. "We just have to take what we are, where we are, and trust God," he said quietly. "Let's go to bed, Jeff."

2
The Battle Begins

Breakfast the next morning was rather strange. Leah got up expecting to fix her usual fare of bacon, eggs, and biscuits. Instead she found, to her surprise, Jeff standing in front of the stove.

"What are you doing, Jeff?"

"Fixing breakfast." He was wearing a white cotton shirt and a pair of worn trousers in place of his uniform. "This time I'll be the cook," he announced. "You can make the coffee if you want to."

Leah looked at the bowl of frog legs sitting on the counter next to the stove. "I'm not going to eat any of those ole things!" she proclaimed.

"It's that or nothing," he said with a grin. "You'll like them. Sit down and watch an expert."

So Leah sat and watched as Jeff began cooking the frog legs. It was really like frying chicken, she thought.

Uncle Silas came in, followed by Tom and Jeff's father.

Tom said, "Well, this looks good. I'll just help you set the table, Jeff, and make the coffee." He busied himself.

And soon the meal was ready.

Jeff put the huge platter of frog legs on the table, along with a large tray of biscuits that he had warmed in the oven. He glanced at Leah with a mischievous look as he sat down. "Why don't you ask the blessing, Leah?" he asked innocently. "And be sure you give a special thanks to the Lord for these frog legs."

Leah flushed and shook her head stubbornly. "I won't do it! I'm thankful for almost anything but not those old frog legs!"

"I'll do it," Tom said cheerfully. He asked a simple blessing—paying special heed to the frog legs—and when he said, "Amen," he reached out and speared one of the succulent legs from the platter. Grabbing a biscuit in his left hand, he began to take alternate bites. "Boy, this is good! Nothing like good, fresh frog legs for breakfast!"

The men all were grinning as they ate. Leah saw they were watching her. She sat bolt upright, her lips set in a stubborn line.

Finally Silas said, "Just try one, Leah. It won't kill you."

Leah looked at him and then sniffed. "Well, all right, but just one." She picked up a frog leg from the platter and took a small bite. She took another bite.

"It's good, isn't it? I told you it would be," Jeff said. "Just jump in now and eat all you want.

Leah found, to her surprise, that she really did like frog legs. They tasted a little like chicken and a little like fish.

"Now every time you want a good meal, all you have to do is go out and gig you a frog," Jeff said.

"No, I wouldn't stick that gig into a frog or anything else."

"You're not as tenderhearted toward the chickens though," Jeff teased. "I've seen you wring the neck of many a fine bird."

"Chickens are different," Leah argued. "Anyway, I'm not gigging any old frogs."

After the meal, she cleaned up, and soon afterward Lt. Majors and Tom took their leave.

"We've got to get back to camp," the lieutenant said. "We sure appreciate that good meal, Leah. You're a fine cook." He turned to Silas. "Thanks for having us out."

Jeff said, rather formally, "Let me stay another night, will you, Lieutenant? I don't have anything to do when I get back to camp. Maybe I can go hunting and get some rabbits for Mr. Carter."

His father glanced at Leah, cocking his head to one side. He looked back at Jeff and looked about to tease the boy but must have decided better of it. "If it's all right with Mr. Carter, it's all right with me," he said. "As long as you're back tomorrow."

"Let the boy stay." Silas nodded. "Some fresh jackrabbit would go down pretty good."

"All right then."

Lt. Majors and Tom said their good-byes and went out and climbed into the wagon. Jeff and Leah came outside and waved as they disappeared.

"Can I go hunting with you, Jeff?"

"Why, sure. It'll be like old times. But first I've got to teach your Uncle Silas who's the best checker player." He went back inside and challenged his host. "I'm ready to show you how to be a real checker player, Mr. Carter."

"All right, we'll see about that."

Uncle Silas set up a board on the kitchen table, and soon the two were deeply engaged in a fierce battle.

Leah was amused at the seriousness with which Jeff took the game. When he made an especially good move, he would pound the table, making the checkers jump up and down, and shout, "Yahoo!" On the other hand, when Silas jumped one or two of his men, Jeff would scowl and hunch down in his chair as if preparing to make a bayonet charge.

Finally at midmorning the game was interrupted when someone called out, "Hello, is anyone home?"

Leah went to the door and saw a young neighbor outside, Rafe Tolliver. He was sixteen years old—and she had thought at times that he was fond of her. "Come in, Rafe," she invited.

Rafe Tolliver was tall with blond hair and light blue eyes. He looked Leah over, then said, "Hi, Jeff. Are you giving him a good thrashing?"

Silas grinned. "I've beat him three out of five. I guess that makes me the champion."

"No, it don't," Jeff argued heatedly. "We're going to play the best eight out of ten."

Rafe winked at Leah, saying, "After they settle which one of them is best, *I'll* teach them how to play checkers."

"What are you doing today, Rafe?"

"I'm going hunting after chores. I've got my dog all ready. I expect I'll get me a mess of coons."

Jeff looked up quickly. "I'd like to go, Rafe, if I wouldn't be in the way."

"Why, shoot! You can't get too many people out on a coon hunt." Rafe grinned. He obviously liked Jeff. Then he looked over at Leah and said, "If you'll get out of that dress and into your old overalls, I'll let you go too. What're you all dressed up for?"

Leah felt her face flush. She had put on her second-best dress, a light yellow affair with white

26

daisies crocheted across the front. "Oh, I just like to wear a nice dress every once in a while."

"She wears it when she eats frog legs." Uncle Silas grinned slyly. "I'll bet she'd wear it for some good fried coon, wouldn't you, Leah?"

Leah turned and walked away, saying, "Oh, you hush, Uncle Silas!"

Rafe said, "I guess we'll go about dusk tonight. I've got my chores to do. Come on over to our place about six. Better bring some grub too, Leah. We're liable to get hungry out there."

"Rafe's a pretty nice fellow, isn't he?" Jeff asked Leah after the boy left.

"Oh, yes, he is. He helps Uncle Silas sometimes with things only a man can do."

"I thought you could do anything a man could do," he teased. Then he threw up both hands. "Wait a minute! Don't shoot! I was just kidding." He looked out the window and watched Rafe disappear into the distance. "I think he's kind of sweet on you. He looked like it to me."

"Don't be silly!"

"I'm not being silly. Just shows he has good taste."

Leah shot a look at Jeff, then blushed. "I don't know about that. He's a nice boy, though." She changed the subject, saying, "If we're going to go hunting, I'll need to get all my work done too. Why don't you go out there and work on that woodpile? Uncle Silas will be needing at least two or three cords this winter."

"All right, I'll do that."

* * *

"Well, how do you like this new dog of mine?" Rafe asked, putting his hand proudly on the head of a large coonhound.

"He looks good. What is he?"

"This here's a black-and-tan. Best coon dog in the world!"

The dog's fur was black with a bluish tinge, except for his muzzle and feet. These were soft brown like a fine suede jacket. He had a glossy coat and clear bright eyes. He held his tail above his back, and he looked wide awake, not tired like some dogs.

"He weighs over fifty pounds. Look at those muscles on him!"

"What's his name?" Leah asked.

"His name's Stonewall, named after the general."

"You can't get a name better than that." Jeff grinned. He put his hand out, and the dog sniffed, then licked it. "Sure is a fine dog. Is he good with coons?"

"Good with coons? Of course he is. Why, I wouldn't have a dog that wouldn't get a coon," Rafe said indignantly.

"Is he fast?" Jeff demanded.

"Well, he's fast enough." Rafe shrugged. "Fastest dog's a greyhound. But what would one of them things be worth on a coon hunt? Nothing! What counts is smarts. A dog's either smart or dumb. You can teach him lots of things, but you can't teach him sense. Either he's got it," Rafe pronounced, "or he ain't got it. You two about ready to go?"

Jeff nodded, and they left the house. A big moon was shining, and far off the barking of dogs sounded

28

like bells. "Somebody else out hunting," Jeff remarked.

"Yep, but they ain't got no Stonewall dog like we got."

They made their way along the road for awhile, then turned into the deep woods. They walked for what seemed hours to Leah, the two boys chatting from time to time. They seemed to have forgotten her, which made her feel a little left out. *I wish it was just Jeff and me on this coon hunt,* she thought. *Those two won't do anything but talk about dogs all night long.*

The moon was rising quickly, and all of a sudden Stonewall let out a strange sound. It was half bark and half howl. He was somewhere up ahead, and Rafe said excitedly, "That's a coon!"

"How do you know? Maybe it's a possum."

Rafe began to run, but he shouted disgustedly, "Why, Stonewall would die of shame if he ever took out after a possum! He knows he's a coon dog, not a possum dog."

They ran hard as the dog bayed, and they finally reached a big tree with Stonewall at the bottom. "He's got one treed all right, but I can't see it. We'll have to wait a while here. Maybe build a fire so we can see what we're doing."

For a while, they circled the tree, trying to see through the darkness. But none of them could spot a coon.

"You know what I think?" Rafe said suddenly.

"What's that, Rafe?" Leah asked.

"Look how close these trees are together. I think that ole coon went up this tree"—he pointed upward, moving his arm—"climbed out on one of those limbs, and jumped into another tree and then maybe another tree."

Jeff looked around. "I've known coons to do that, all right. I had me a dog back in Kentucky named Rocky. You know, he knew how to mark a tree. He'd figure out that the critter must've gone to another tree, and he'd start searching until he found Mr. Coon, maybe just coming down."

"Ain't no dog that smart," Rafe said.

"Rocky was. Anyhow, let's kind of spread out. There ain't nothing up in this tree."

Sure enough, the dog struck a scent some hundred yards away.

"Told you," Jeff said. "He got out of that first tree. Let's get him."

Evidently the coon was smarter than any of them and even smarter than the dog, for they could not catch him.

Finally Leah was out of breath and tired. "I can't go much farther," she panted.

Jeff must have seen that she was about past going. "Me too. Let's build a fire, Rafe. We'll eat something, then go after him again."

"All right," Rafe agreed.

They set about finding an open spot. The boys quickly found enough dead wood to make a fire, and soon a merry crackling blaze drove the darkness back. They sat down, and Leah opened the sack they had taken turns carrying.

"I'm hungry," she announced.

"What've you got in there?" Rafe demanded. "Whatever it is, it'll be good."

Leah began pulling out food and handing it off. "Well, here's some cold fried chicken—and here's some frog legs we had left. Jeff, you liked them so much, you can have all of them. Here's some baked potatoes and some biscuits."

"Let me have some of all of it," Jeff said.

They sat around the fire eating, quickly at first, then slowing down. When they were full, Leah said, "That's all, except for some fried pies.'

Jeff sat up straight. "Fried *apple* pies?"

"Yes. I hid them from you and your greedy relatives.'

"Gimme!" Jeff held out his hand.

"There's only three of them. Just one apiece."

"Well, let me eat yours. You don't like them much anyway, Leah."

"I do so!" she said offendedly. "Don't be such a pig."

Jeff took his pie and sat back. "I'll give you all my share of the coon, if you'll give me your pie, Rafe."

"Nothing doing. I can catch a coon anytime." Rafe grinned. "But I can't get fried pies like this!"

They ate the pies and then decided they were thirsty.

"There's a creek back a ways, but I'm too tired and full to go get a drink," Jeff said.

"Let's just rest awhile." Leah leaned against a tree. She looked at the fire and said, "I love being out in the woods like this, where it's nice and quiet and with a nice fire."

"Well, you're in good company too." Rafe grinned. "That makes a big difference.

Leah smiled at him and nodded. "It sure does, Rafe."

Rafe glanced at Jeff. "Well, Jeff, you've got to go back to the army, but I'll be sure Leah gets to go coon hunting and maybe trout lining once in a while.

Jeff gave him an angry look but said nothing.

They sat talking, letting the sounds of the night filter through to them. And finally Rafe lay back and soon began to snore.

"He sounds like a sawmill!" Jeff exclaimed. "I don't see how anybody could sleep in the same house with him."

"He *is* loud, isn't he?" Leah giggled. She looked over to where the young man was lying on his back, his mouth wide open. "It'd be mean if I found a bug and dropped it in there, wouldn't it?"

"It might be fun. Do you want to do it?"

"No, he might get mad."

"We could tell him that it fell out of a tree," Jeff suggested.

"No, it would be mean. You wouldn't want someone to do that to you, would you?"

"It's been worse in camp. They pull some awful tricks on us young fellas—the older soldiers do."

The fire crackled, and Jeff reached over and put a few more sticks on it. As he stirred them, the sparks swirled high into the air. He said, "It looks like those sparks are mingling with the stars, don't it, Leah?"

Leah looked up and saw indeed that the white cold stars were all mixed up with the hot flaming sparks. "One of my teachers told me those stars are on fire. They don't look it, do they?"

"No, they don't. They look like icy points, real cold. But they do flicker sometimes. They last a little bit longer than those sparks, though."

"I wish I knew all their names—all those stars, I mean."

"Pa knows a lot of them," Jeff said. "He taught me some. That right up there—see it—that real bright one? That one's called Sirius. Pretty, isn't it?"

"Serious? How could a star be serious?"

"I don't know. That's just what Pa said. Look! There's the Big Dipper. See?"

"I can't see it. Never could pick it out."

Jeff came over and sat down. He put his hand on her head and put his face next to hers. "Now look—right where I'm pointing your head—" He held her head steady, then released one hand and put his arm out. "Right along my arm. Just take a sight. It looks like a dipper turned upside down."

"I don't see a thing."

Jeff shook his head. "Look! See that star, those four—they make the cup of the dipper. The other part is bent over."

"I see it! I see it!" Leah suddenly turned, and her eyes were beaming with pleasure. "First time I could ever pick it out. Oh, Jeff, that's exciting!"

Jeff grinned at her and leaned back. "You're not hard to entertain. I've been seeing the Big Dipper all my life. I thought everybody did."

They both fell quiet for awhile, and finally Leah said, "I think a lot about those days when we were growing up back home."

"So do I." Jeff hesitated. "Pa says we can never have that time again."

"We can go back there after the war's over."

"I don't know about that." Jeff shrugged. "Even if we did, we'll be old."

"Old?" Leah stared at him with shock. "What do you mean, old?"

"Well, just look at it. If the war lasts another two or three years, we'll be nearly eighteen, nineteen years old. That's old."

"That's not old. Sarah's eighteen, and Tom's nineteen, and they're not old."

Jeff picked up a stick and began to dig in the dirt with it. "Maybe not. But when you're fifteen, nineteen seems old. Why, when you're that old, you have to get married, have a family, and work all the time!"

"Well, that's the way it is," Leah protested. "What else would you do?"

Jeff grinned at her. "I'd like to be rich and have people wait on me all the time, get everything I want, and go where I want to go."

Leah laughed aloud at him. "That's silly! You wouldn't like that."

"Wouldn't mind trying it for awhile." Jeff shrugged. "Might beat working."

"I think about Tom and Sarah a lot. I wish they would get married, but of course they can't while the war's on."

"Tom's really sad. He doesn't show it much, but he thinks about Sarah all the time."

"Does he ever talk to you about her?"

"One time he did. It was just before the battle at Bull Run—the night before, as a matter of fact. We were sitting around talking and thinking about it, and all of a sudden Tom said, 'If I get killed, I'll miss it all.' I asked him what that meant, and he said, 'Never get married, never have children, never watch them grow up—miss it all.'"

He turned to Leah. "It really made me sad. That was the first time I saw how grieved Tom was to not be able to marry your sister."

34

"I think Sarah feels the same. She writes about Tom, and I can tell she's hurting on the inside."

"Well, we don't have to worry about that since you're fourteen and I'm fifteen," Jeff said. "I don't want to get married till I'm real old, maybe twenty-five."

Leah said, "Why, I know girls that get married when they're only fifteen. Just a year older than I am."

"That what's on your mind—getting married next year?" Jeff teased.

Rafe suddenly erupted with an enormous burst of sound, and she glanced over at him.

"Maybe you ought to marry Rafe there." Jeff grinned. "You wouldn't have to worry about sleeping much. I swear, he'd keep the regiment awake!"

They kept on talking, and for Leah it was a time of peace and relaxation. They had been so caught up with the war and the hardships that she treasured moments like these.

Rafe snorted, then sat up abruptly. He rubbed his eyes and looked around. "Well, were you going to let me sleep all night?" he demanded. He got to his feet, stretched hugely, and said, "Let's go get them coons."

They did get a coon later that night. Stonewall treed it, and Rafe shot it out of the tree.

As it fell to the ground and lay still, the dog yapped around it excitedly.

"Get away from there, Stonewall!" Rafe commanded. He carefully poked the raccoon with the muzzle of his rifle. "A big, fat one!" he said with satisfaction. "Probably been eating on somebody's corn."

"It's too early for corn." Carefully Jeff reached out and picked the animal up by its tail. His eyes widened, and he said, "Why, this coon must weigh thirty pounds!"

"He's a good'un," Rafe said. "You want to try for another one?"

"Not me. I've got to get back. I've got to leave for camp this morning."

"All right. Come on, Stonewall."

The two boys took turns carrying the heavy coon, and Leah carried the gun. When they got back to Rafe's house, she watched as he expertly cleaned the animal and divided it.

"Take this and cook it up for your Uncle Silas. He's partial to some fresh coon. Be sure and cook some sweet potatoes with it. That goes down pretty good."

Jeff came over and put out his hand. "Thanks a lot for letting us go with you, Rafe. That's a fine dog you got there. I hope I have one as good one of these days."

"I hope you will." Rafe hesitated, then said, "You be careful, Jeff, when that battle starts. Don't want nothing to happen to you."

Jeff and Leah walked away from the Tolliver place, and on the way back Jeff said, "I like Rafe."

"So do I."

"I reckon he'll be in the army soon. He's sixteen now. We've got fellas younger than that. I expect he'll join up."

The thought depressed Leah. "It seems like everybody has to suffer in this war—all the young men, and then the mothers and sisters have to stay home and worry."

There was nothing to say to that.

Suddenly Jeff stopped. "What was that?"

Leah halted too. They stood there in the bright moonlight and listened. "Thunder, I think."

But Jeff shook his head. "That's not thunder—that's artillery. Way off over there." He strained his eyes, then shook his head. "Too far away to see the powder flashes, but I've heard it enough to know that's what it is."

They went into the house and found that Silas was already up and stirring around. He liked to get up early, and when Leah produced the coon, he was pleased. "That'll go down all right," he said.

Jeff said, "I've got to get back." He paused, then told Uncle Silas, "The battle's starting. I hear the guns."

His leaving was a sad time for all three of them.

Leah had prepared a huge box of cookies for Jeff to take back to share with the rest of his company. After he said good-bye to Silas, she walked out with him and handed him the box, saying, "Be sure Tom and your father get some of these. And the rest of the company too—your friends."

"I'll see to that." Jeff hesitated longer and finally burst out, "I sure hate to go, Leah! I surely do!"

They stood facing each other, torn by the grief that came at times like this, and finally he said awkwardly, "Well, I guess I've got to go." He put out his hand, and she took it. Trying to grin, he said, "We had us a good time, didn't we? Your first frog legs and that fine coon hunt!"

"Yes, we did." Leah's voice was so quiet, she knew he could hardly hear it.

He pulled his hand back, turned, and started walking toward the road. "I'll get me a ride," he called back. "Somebody's bound to be going toward Richmond. Good-bye, Leah."

"Good-bye, Jeff. Be careful." She watched until he was out of sight, then walked back into the house.

She was quiet all morning, and finally, as the sound of artillery grew louder, her uncle said, "Lee's gone up against the Yankees. I think it'll be a bad one."

"The South won before—at Bull Run."

Uncle Silas looked in the direction of Richmond, then turned to her, and his face was drawn and serious. "I don't think they'll be whipped that easy this time."

Leah came and put her arms around him. She was crying.

He put his arms around her, and she clung to him. He finally murmured, "God be with them all!"

3

After the Battle

Ordinarily in Richmond, Independence Day would have been gaily celebrated. There would have been flags flying, fireworks, a dance in the city square, and every home would have celebrated the birth of America. However on July 4, 1862, there was little evidence of festivity.

Leah Carter left Uncle Silas's house and made her way to the heart of the city early in the morning. She was somewhat worried about her uncle. He had been ill but had done better until very recently. Now he had taken a cold, and it had settled in his chest so that he was coughing a great deal.

Leah thought, *I wish Sarah hadn't had to go back to Kentucky. I miss her, and so does Uncle Silas.*

The two girls had come to Richmond to take care of their uncle, but Sarah had incurred the anger and suspicion of some of the authorities. Since they were from Kentucky, a border state, they had not been warmly welcomed into the Confederacy in any case.

"Hello, Mrs. Lake," Leah said as she stepped into the store and approached the counter. "I need some coffee and sugar, please."

Mrs. Lake, a tall angular woman, shook her head. "Laws, child! We haven't had any *real* coffee in a week now, nor are we likely to get any."

Leah's face fell. "Uncle Silas has to have his coffee!" she protested. "I'll go try down the street."

"You can go, but I doubt if you'll find any. The blockade's got us cut off so tightly now that coffee's just one of the things we're going to have to learn how to do without." Mrs. Lake shook her head sadly. "Maybe you can roast acorns and grind them up. That's what some are doing."

Leah made a face. "That doesn't sound very good. I think I'll try a few more stores. Thank you, Mrs. Lake."

She visited four other groceries, finally finding the items she sought. But when she heard the price of a pound of coffee, she blinked. "I never heard of such for coffee!"

Nevertheless, it was all she could find, so she bought it.

As she returned through the streets of Richmond, she noticed a great deal of activity. Men and women were talking, some of the men rather loudly, and soldiers were everywhere.

Since McClellan's Northern army had landed and made its way almost to the outskirts of Richmond, the far-off sound of cannon and even musket fire could be heard. The Confederates had lost their foremost general, Joseph Johnston, and General Robert E. Lee had been placed in command.

Leah was at the end of the main road and had started to turn toward her uncle's house when she saw two soldiers approaching, carrying a stretcher.

They stopped as they came close to her, put down the stretcher, and just sat down in the road, gasping for breath.

"It's a good thing we got this far," the older of the two panted, "but I don't know what we're going to do with him."

The other, no more than eighteen, was trembling with fatigue. "I don't either," he said. "If something doesn't turn up, we'll just have to find a tent."

Leah paused. She looked down at the wounded man on the stretcher and then swallowed hard. Some dreadful blow had torn his arm off, and the stump was bound with a bloody cloth. His mouth was open, and he was breathing shallowly. His skin was pale gray.

"The hospital in Chimborazo. Can't you take him there?" she asked timidly.

"No, missy." The older man shook his head wearily. "We just come from there. Every room's full, and they got wounded men all over the grass outside." He looked down at the wounded boy. "We got to do something, but for the life of me I don't know what."

Leah felt slightly sick at the sight of the terrible wound. She watched as the two men got to their feet, heaved the stretcher up, and staggered away.

On her way home she met wagon after wagon full of groaning men. One of them was crying out, "Let me die! It's killing me, this jolting! Put me out and let me die!"

By the time she reached home, she was totally bewildered.

Walking into the house, Leah found Uncle Silas sitting in his rocking chair, reading his Bible. Silas Carter was the brother of Leah's father, Dan. He had been near death when his two nieces came to nurse him, and he had grown very fond of both of them.

41

"Uncle Silas," she said, "the wounded are coming back from the battle, and there's no place to put them. The hospital's full." Then she related what she had heard from the two soldiers.

"I just don't know what we could do," he said sadly. He shook his head and stroked his gray beard. "I've heard that thousands of them have died. Mrs. Rayburn came by for a while. She says she'd never seen anything like it. They're busy digging graves and burying them, Yank and Confederate alike. I just don't know, Leah. It's terrible!"

For two more days the wounded continued to stream into Richmond.

Then late one afternoon a knock came at the door, and Leah went to open it.

"Jeff!" she said, smiling. She took the arm of the tall young man in gray uniform who stood there and pulled him into the house. "Come on in. I just made an apple pie."

"An apple pie! Well, I reckon I could arm wrestle a piece of that down my throat."

Jeff Majors was fifteen. His hair was as black as a crow, and his eyes were black also. He was called "The Black Majors" by some of the family because of this. He allowed himself to be pulled into the kitchen and sat down in a cane-bottom chair. When Leah put a piece of steaming pie before him, he threw himself into it.

"Don't eat so fast, Jeff! You'll burn your tongue!" she warned. She moved to the stove, picked up the coffeepot, poured a half cup, then set it before him. "I wish I could give you more, but the coffee's almost gone. And it's about impossible to find."

Jeff swallowed an enormous bite, then nodded. "Yep, so I heard. How is your Uncle Silas?"

"He's better now. He had a cold, but he's about over it."

Leah sat down across from him. She was fourteen years old. She had green eyes and blonde hair and was very tall for a girl. She saw herself as being gawky and awkward, and once, when she had developed a stoop to try to appear smaller, her mother had scolded her. "Straighten up, Leah. You look like a worm, all bent over. God gave you a good, strong, tall body. Don't be ashamed of it."

She was wearing a light blue dress today, and a green ribbon tied her hair back.

Jeff didn't say so, but he thought she looked very pretty.

"Jeff, it's terrible!" she exclaimed. "All these wounded men—what's going to happen to them?"

He frowned, and a sober look touched his dark eyes. "I guess some of them are going to die. A lot of them already have."

"The hospital's full, they say, and there's not enough medicine or bandages or anything."

"Well, nine men in our company alone are lying out under a tree," Jeff murmured. He sipped his coffee slowly, then frowned again. "We took some canvas and made a tent so it won't rain on them. But they're just lying there with no doctor. I don't know what'll happen."

He sat with his long legs stuck out in front of him, and the two talked for a long time.

Both had lived in the little town of Pineville, Kentucky, until the war came. Jeff's parents decided they could not fight against their native state, Virginia, so Nelson Majors and his wife and their two boys, Tom and Jeff, left for Richmond. Then Mrs. Majors died giving birth to a baby girl, Esther. Since the Majors men had no one to care for her, they were relieved when Leah's parents volunteered to keep the baby until her father could find better arrangements.

After Jeff went back to camp that afternoon, Leah kept thinking about the the poor wounded and dying men in Richmond.

That night after supper, Silas got out his Bible as usual. He began to read in the book of James, while Leah sat knitting a sock, listening carefully. She had learned to treasure her uncle, who was as fervent a Christian as her own father.

Silas finally reached the fourteenth verse of the second chapter. He read very slowly. "If a brother or sister be naked, and destitute of daily food, and one of you say unto them, depart in peace, be ye warmed and filled; notwithstanding ye give them not those things which are needful to the body; what doth it profit?" He hesitated, his lips moved as he silently re-read the question, and then he continued, "Even so faith, if it hath not works, is dead, being alone."

The clock from the hall was making a rhythmical ticking, *tick-tock, tick-tock.* Leah looked up from her knitting to see that her uncle's eyes were troubled. "What is it, Uncle Silas?"

"That verse, it seems to speak to my heart, Leah," he said. "Let's pray for all the wounded men. Pray that God would show us how to help them."

They had a time of prayer in which they prayed for the wounded of both armies. Leah prayed fervently for her brother, Royal, who was with the North. They prayed also for Jeff, and for Tom, Jeff's brother, and for their father, who were serving in the Southern army.

They finally went to bed.

The next morning, Silas seemed preoccupied. He ate the corn mush and biscuits that Leah set out for him and sipped his coffee slowly. Looking up, he said finally, "I've got a place out in the country, Leah, about three miles out of town. Richmond Manor, we used to call it. Not much of a house, on a couple of acres. I used to keep milk cows out there and goats. The place is run down, but it's livable."

"I never knew that, Uncle Silas."

"Well, the Lord spoke to me right smartly. We're going to let the army use this place here. It's close to the hospital, and we'll live out at Richmond Manor."

Leah's face brightened, "Oh, Uncle Silas! That's wonderful! The soldiers will have beds here, and they'll be out of the weather! But are you sure it'll be all right for you?"

"Oh, I feel fine." Silas smiled. "I'll feel even better if we can do this for those poor boys. It'll take some moving, but we'll make it. You better start getting packed, and we'll have to get Lem to hitch the team and haul out the stuff we'll need in the wagon. We'll have to take some mattresses probably. And food. There's nothing there."

"Oh, it'll be fun—a little like camping out!" Leah exclaimed.

It took a day for them to make their preparations, but the next morning they left Richmond, headed for the country. The sun was shining. The robins were digging industriously for worms along the wayside. And Leah was happy to be doing something for the soldiers.

As they pulled up over a ridge, Silas nodded. "There it is, back off the road. There's Richmond Manor. Needs a little paint, but that's not important." He hesitated, then said, "There's one thing I didn't tell you about the house."

"What's that, Uncle Silas?"

Silas shrugged his thin shoulders. "Well, some people in the neighborhood say it's haunted."

"Haunted! You don't believe that, do you?"

"No, of course I don't, child. But a man killed his wife there thirty years ago—long before I bought the place. People passing along the road claim they can still hear the woman crying. Nonsense, of course." He looked around. "We could get a cow, and we don't mind a few ghosts, do we, Leah?"

4

A Haunted House

Settling into the house in the country was much simpler than Leah had thought. When she and Silas first stepped inside Richmond Manor, she had been appalled by the condition of the old place. Dust was everywhere. The windows were so filthy it was almost impossible to see out, and the furniture was in poor condition.

They made the best of it on the first night, but at ten o'clock the next morning Tom and Jeff Majors came riding up.

Leah saw them through the window. "Look, Uncle Silas—it's Tom and Jeff!"

They stepped out onto the porch, and the two soldiers dismounted and tied their horses. Both boys were grinning widely. "Our dad got a promotion," Jeff said proudly. "He's been made a captain."

Tom took off his hat and knocked the dust from it. He was tall and dark like Jeff and wore the uniform of a sergeant. "The first order he gave was, 'Go help Miss Leah and her uncle make that place fit to live in.'"

"Well, that was right nice of your pa." Uncle Silas beamed. He looked around and said, "Quite a bit of work to do around here."

Jeff nodded to Leah. "Make us another one of them apple pies," he said, "and just watch our smoke."

Later he told her, "Pa was really pleased that you and your uncle have made your house available to our men. I think it's fine too."

"Oh, it's what we should do," Leah said quickly. She smiled and touched the locket that hung from a gold chain around her neck. "And I love my locket. That's the best birthday present I ever got."

Jeff shrugged. "Well, a girl ought to have something pretty like that. I'm glad you like it."

Later on she prepared a fine dinner—including apple pie.

As they were eating, Tom said, "Did you hear what happened in the North—what Lincoln's done?"

"No, what's that, Sergeant?" Silas asked.

"Well, Lincoln's called for three hundred thousand men to serve for three years." He took a bite of pork chop and chewed on it thoughtfully. "Three hundred thousand men! I expect that's more than we've got in the whole South. And to serve for *three years. . . .*"

"I guess most of our fellows will serve as long as the war will last. But that can't be three years!" Jeff said.

The two soldiers worked hard all day, and at dusk Tom said, "Well, we've got to get back to camp. Come along, Jeff."

Jeff lingered long enough to say, "I'll be coming back from time to time, Leah. It looks like the fighting's over for a while. McClellan's retreated, gone back to Washington, so maybe we'll get to see each other. Maybe there's a creek around here or a pond we can go fishing in."

"Oh, that would be nice, Jeff. You be sure and come every chance you get."

The next day Leah said, "Uncle Silas, I've got to have some more groceries. I saw a little store down the road. I'm going to walk down and get some things."

It was a good day for walking. The sky was blue, and white clouds drifted across it. The grass was so green it almost hurt her eyes. Once she crossed a bridge that arched over a small creek. She stopped and leaned out over it and looked down into the depths, hoping to see fish, but all she saw was shiny minnows schooling over the shallow water.

Finally she walked on and came to the one-room store with a little house sitting behind it.

"My name's Leah Carter," she said. "My Uncle Silas and I are living down the road. We'll be needing groceries from time to time."

The couple behind the counter looked at her strangely, she thought.

"Well," the man said, "my name's Henry Wiggins. My wife, Pearl. Glad to have you in the community."

Mrs. Wiggins asked, *"Which* house did you say you lived in?"

"The one just on the other side of the rise, sitting out in the field under the cottonwood trees."

"Oh," Mrs. Wiggins said shortly. She gave Leah a peculiar look but said no more.

"What can I help you with, miss?" Mr. Wiggins said. He moved about, picking up the few items she asked for. "We don't have any coffee." He shook his head. "Don't know where you'll get that." He added up the items and said, "That'll come to two dollars and sixteen cents."

Leah paid for the groceries and picked them up. "It's nice out here. I like it out in the country, and it's really a nice house now that we're getting it fixed up."

Mrs. Wiggins was a large woman and had a round face. Her mouth grew tight. "Well, I hope you'll be all right there."

Leah noted the strange expression on her face. "Well, of course we'll be all right there. Why wouldn't we?"

Mrs. Wiggins sniffed. She picked up a can of snuff and filled her lower lip, then said tartly, "Well, *I* wouldn't spend one night in that place!"

"Now, Emmy," Mr. Wiggins said quickly, "don't be saying things like that."

"Henry, you know that place's haunted. I tell you, I wouldn't stay there for ten minutes."

But Mr. Wiggins shushed her up. "You come back, Miss Leah, and tell your uncle to drop by too. We're glad to have you in the neighborhood."

When Leah returned to the house, she told Uncle Silas about the conversation.

But he merely smiled. "Folks are real superstitious. You're not afraid, are you, Leah?"

"No, I don't believe in ghosts."

Two days went by, and by that time they were comfortably settled. Leah had worked hard on the house so that it was clean as a pin. They bought five hens from Mr. Wiggins, who also had a farm, and they hoped to get a milk cow soon.

"This is real nice out here, isn't it, Uncle? So much quieter than it is in town."

She was sitting in a rocking chair on the front porch, across from Uncle Silas. He was reading a newspaper, and he looked up to say, "Yes, I like this country air." Then he studied the paper carefully. "Listen to this, Leah. It says, 'General Nathan Bedford Forrest has captured Murfreesboro. General Forrest captured 880 Federal prisoners, including an entire Michigan regiment.'" He looked up. "Now, that's something, isn't it! That Forrest must be *some* general."

And they talked about the war.

That night after they had had their Bible reading, Leah went to bed. She slept poorly for some reason, tossing and turning on the cotton mattress. Finally, she dozed off—or almost so.

As she lay there, not quite awake yet not asleep either, she thought she heard something. At first she thought it was something outside, but then it seemed that footsteps, very faint, were coming from somewhere in the house.

She lay still, listening, and she thought, *I've been hearing too many stories about haunted houses. There's no such thing.*

She went to sleep finally, and the next morning at breakfast she told her uncle.

"I guess I'm getting nervous," she said. "I thought I heard footsteps in the house last night, but I know that couldn't be."

Silas glanced up. "Well, whoever it was, you can shoot him with my pistol. If it's a ghost, it won't hurt him, will it?"

Leah thought no more about it and that day took some time to go for a walk. She did find a creek close by that looked as if it might be full of plump fish, and she resolved to come back and see if she could catch any.

51

She went home and began to prepare supper, but when she reached into the potato bin, she stopped suddenly, staring at the potatoes. "Why, I *know* there were four potatoes here. I put them in yesterday. Now there are only three." Slowly she closed the lid and cooked supper, deciding she had made a mistake.

Later though, when going to bed, Leah was still thinking about the missing potato. "I know I can count to four," she said to herself as she put on her gown and got in between the thick blankets. She lay listening to the wind rising. A summer storm was coming. "Maybe Uncle Silas ate it, although I can't imagine him eating a raw potato."

In the middle of the night, Leah awoke, filled with terror.

Something was touching her back!

Without thinking she let out a wild scream and jumped out of bed. She ran down the hall into the living room, her heart pounding, and soon Uncle Silas came stomping out of his room, carrying a candle and trying to pull his robe about him.

"What's the matter?" he demanded.

"Something—something was in my room! It touched my back!"

Silas cocked an eyebrow at her, then walked over to a desk and opened the drawer. He set down the candle, pulled out a huge pistol, and cocked it. Then picking up the candle, he said, "We'll see."

Leah followed closely behind her uncle as they went down the hall. She had slammed the bedroom door behind her, and he opened it and stepped inside. Leah was right behind him. She looked around wildly, and then Uncle Silas laughed.

"Well, there's your ghost, or your burglar, whatever you thought it was," he said.

Leah saw the old calico cat, Peanuts, sitting on her bed. He yawned, showing enormous teeth, as cats do, then curled down and went to sleep.

Uncle Silas took the pistol off cock and patted Leah on the shoulder. "It's all right. A thing like that would have scared me too, getting touched in the back in the dark. You want me to put Peanuts out?"

"No, it's all right, now that I know he's here. You go on back to bed, Uncle Silas. I'm sorry I woke you up. Good night!"

"Good night!"

Leah walked to the window and looked out. The trees were tossing, but she saw nothing else. Then she got back into bed, and Peanuts came and touched her hair tentatively with one paw.

"Leave me alone," she said crossly. But she picked him up and held him close, finding comfort in the warm, furry body.

She closed her eyes and tried to go to sleep. The wind blew, making a high-pitched sound, and the apple tree outside her window seemed to lean over and scratch on the glass with skeleton fingers.

5
Midnight Visitor

Leah and Silas enjoyed their stay in Richmond Manor. When the neighbors came by to visit, though, both of them sensed they were apprehensive.

"Some of them really do believe in ghosts, don't they?" Leah asked.

"Oh, yes, some people are like that," Uncle Silas agreed.

She said suddenly, "Uncle Silas, did you take two of the fried pies that I made yesterday?"

"Why, I had some for supper."

"No, I mean did you get up last night and eat any?" She had a puzzled look on her face. "I know I left ten of them in the pie safe, and when I looked a while ago there were only eight."

Silas stared at her. "Well, not guilty. They were good enough to eat, though. You probably didn't count right."

"I suppose so. Or I may have gotten hungry and eaten them in my sleep."

What Leah did not tell her uncle was that she had missed several other items of food also. She had not kept up with them exactly, but somehow she felt that someone was taking things.

"It's not a ghost," she said to herself. "But if somebody's stealing from us, I'm going to do something about it!"

That night after Uncle Silas went to bed, Leah tiptoed into the living room, opened the drawer of the desk, and pulled out the big pistol. It was so heavy she had to hold it with both hands.

Going back into her room, she put it on the table beside her bed and blew out the light. The windows were open, for it was a warm night, and she sat down in a chair and waited. Outside the crickets were making their tiny cries, and far off in the pond she heard a huge bullfrog booming.

Time passed slowly, and twice she nodded off. She came awake abruptly both times, saying to herself, *Here, you've got to do better than that!*

She entertained herself then by thinking of the times she and Jeff had gone hunting for birds' eggs back in Kentucky, and she tried to name as many of the varieties they had found as she could. The night was still, and she was saying, "Redheaded woodpecker, barn sparrow, bluebird—" when suddenly she *knew* she heard something!

Was somebody on the porch? Was that the door opening? Fright came over her, but she held her lips tightly together. If somebody was getting into the house, she had to find out about it.

Carefully she rose, moved to the table, and picked up the pistol. She had watched her uncle cock the weapon, and now, holding it with both hands, she pulled the hammer back.

Click!

The sound was so loud that Leah almost dropped the gun. *If it's a burglar, he probably heard that,* she thought grimly. She stood in the silence, waiting, and then again she heard a noise coming from somewhere down the hall.

She swallowed hard, then said to herself, *Come on, Leah, do* something!

She moved barefoot across the room and carefully pulled the door open. It was very dark, but she knew there was no furniture in the hallway. She tiptoed past her uncle's room and then stopped at the kitchen door. She listened hard but could not hear anything.

There was no candle lit, but the full moon flooded the kitchen with silver light. Hands trembling on the gun, she stepped inside.

Nobody! The kitchen was empty.

I must have been dreaming. Still, she had been so *sure!*

She was turning to go when she heard a faint click. She stood stock still, and suddenly her eye caught a motion. The outside door was starting to open!

With both hands on the butt of the pistol, Leah raised it slowly. The door swung back, and there, outlined against the brightness of the night outside, was a man!

"Stop!" she said loudly. "You stop right there, or I'll—I'll shoot!"

The man immediately stopped. She could not see his face, for he wore a hat pulled down low over his eyes.

"Don't you move," she said. "I've got a gun, and I'll use it."

"All right. I'm not moving," the man replied quietly.

Leah moved over to the kitchen table, took a match from the shelf of the kitchen stove, struck it, and lit the candle. It caught at once, and the light cast its feeble gleam on the man before her.

Why, he's only a boy, she thought. But then she saw he was wearing a uniform, a ragged Union uniform.

"You're a Union soldier," she whispered.

He pulled off his hat, and she saw that he was indeed very young, not much older than herself. His face was thin, and he had curly brown hair, which had not been cut recently. She saw, even by the light of the candle, that he appeared flushed.

"Where'd you come from?" she demanded.

"Got away from Belle Isle Prison a while back," he said.

Leah had heard of Belle Isle. It was a terrible place, according to all the stories. Even the Confederates said it was shameful. Men were made to live outside and practically starve. The guards were overly zealous and shot anyone who even looked as if he might escape.

She stood there for a moment, not knowing what to do. "What's your name?" she said kindly.

"Ezra—Ezra Payne."

"You don't look old enough to be a soldier."

He made no reply.

"You've been taking food from our kitchen, haven't you?"

"Yes, ma'am, I have." He made no apology but just stood there.

Leah saw that his hands were shaking. No, his whole body was shaking.

"Why," she took a step closer, "you've got fever!" she exclaimed.

His eyes were sunk back in his head, and he wore only a light shirt, ripped in several places and a pair of tattered trousers.

"I got captured at Bull Run," he murmured, his voice very thin and shaky. "I've been in Belle Isle for nigh onto a year now. Couldn't stand it anymore, so I ran away."

Leah saw that he was swaying, about to fall. "Here!" she said. "Sit down." She shoved a chair at him.

He stared at her for a moment, then sat. "Thank you," he said. "I'm not strong as a kitten. Never felt this bad before."

And Leah had never been so puzzled before. What to do with him? She thought of calling her uncle but instead asked, "You say you've been in prison for a whole year?"

"Yes, ma'am, a whole year, nearly. Lots of times I wished I'd been killed. It'd been a sight easier, I think, than living in that place."

He began to tremble violently and pulled his shirt up closer. His teeth were chattering.

Leah said, "You need to be in bed. Where have you been sleeping?"

"Out in the loft of the barn." He tried to grin. "It's better than what I had at Belle Isle." He began shaking even more violently and said, "Well, you can go get your menfolks. I know what you got to do."

Leah stared at him, hugging her robe closely around her. "It won't be too good for you to go back to that place, will it?"

"Don't matter."

Leah was appalled at the hopelessness in his voice. She said sharply, "Yes! It does matter! Are you hungry?"

"No, ma'am, not much. Just got a chill like— real cold."

She stared at the boy. *He can't be over sixteen or seventeen,* she thought, *and he's so sick.*

Leah was an impulsive girl. She had been rebuked by her parents more than once for making snap decisions. She also knew she made wrong decisions quite often. But now, staring at the poor miserable boy trembling in the chair, she thought, *I can't let him go back to Belle Isle Prison. He'll die.*

"Look, I'm going to help you. You don't need to go back to prison until you get well. Let me get some blankets and some clothes. You've got to get warm. You go on back to the barn. I'll be out in a minute."

The boy stared at her in disbelief. "You mean, you're not gonna turn me in?"

"Not until you get better. Now go on."

Leah turned and left the kitchen. She went to her bedroom, where she picked up two blankets, and then stopped off at a chest on the porch. Some of her uncle's old clothes were there. She found a coat and a pair of pants and some socks. Putting these under her arm, she took the candle and made her way around the house, careful to be very quiet.

When she got to the barn, the boy was standing in front of it.

"Let's see where you're sleeping," she said.

She followed him inside before remembering she'd put the gun down by the chest. If he had noticed, he made no remark. She trailed him up a rickety flight of stairs to the dim loft, and he motioned to a pile of straw. "Been sleeping on that."

Leah said, "There's a cot in the attic of the house. Tomorrow I'll get it down and bring it to you after dark. Early in the morning I'll fix you something to eat and bring it to you."

"I'm not—not very hungry, but I sure am cold."

Leah handed him the clothes. "Put these on and wrap these blankets around you. I've got to go now."

Ezra Payne stared at her. He was still trembling like a blade of grass in the wind, and his teeth chattered, but there was gratitude in his voice. "I sure do thank you, ma'am."

As she made her way back into the house, Leah was thinking, *I guess I'm some kind of a traitor.*

Carefully she closed the back door. She thought once of telling Uncle Silas about the fugitive she was harboring, but, as good as her uncle was, she wasn't sure. He might decide they had to turn him in.

Going back into her bedroom, she took off her robe and got into bed. She lay there a long time thinking about Ezra Payne. *I'll have to get up early and fix him something to eat. Maybe I can find some medicine. I wish I were a better nurse!*

Peanuts came and snuggled against her as usual. She held onto him, smoothing his fur, and she whispered, "I'm not really a traitor, Peanuts. He's so sick, he couldn't do anybody any harm."

6

Why Are You
So Nervous, Leah?

Jeff found his duties at camp very light. He had
become an expert drummer boy and had done good
service at the Battle of Seven Days. His command-
ing officer, General Stonewall Jackson, commended
the entire regiment, and he stopped by to meet
with Jeff's father briefly.

"I remember this young man," he said with a
smile. "Are you coming to any of our revival meet-
ings that we'll be having this summer?"

"Oh, yes, sir, General Jackson, I sure will," Jeff
replied eagerly. He was convinced that Stonewall
Jackson was the best general in the world. He knew
also that if General Jackson was better at anything
than soldiering, it was at praying and getting his
men converted. "I'll be there, right up in front,
sir."

"You got a fine son here, Captain Majors,"
Stonewall said.

The general wore his cap in a peculiar fashion,
pulled down almost over his eyes, and the eyes
themselves were strange. He was called "Old Blue
Light" by most of his troopers. Jeff himself had
seen him once during a battle, and indeed his eyes
did glow almost as if there were fire behind them.
Now, however, they were mild, and he nodded at
the two and left.

"He's a fine soldier, isn't he, Pa? Best general in the whole world, I bet."

"Wouldn't be surprised," Jeff's father replied. He glanced at the boy and said, "What have you heard from Leah and her uncle?"

"Well, not much really."

"Not much doing around camp. Why don't you go see her? Maybe bring me back one of those apple pies she makes so well."

"You mean it, sir?" Jeff cried, his eyes alight. "Can I really go?"

"Yes, Private, and don't forget that pie!" he called loudly as Jeff dashed away.

Leah was washing the dishes, and Jeff was drying them. They had eaten a tasty lunch, and Jeff reminded her, "Don't forget, you've got to let me have a pie to take back to Pa." He wiped a plate carefully, held it up, and examined it. "He likes your pies almost as much as I do." He put the plate on the shelf. "My ma could make good pies. Her best was raisin. She made raisin pies like nobody I ever heard of."

Leah saw the expression on Jeff's face. "You miss her a great deal, don't you, Jeff?"

"Sure do. Won't ever forget her."

"I got a letter from my ma yesterday," Leah said. She was scrubbing a skillet, and a lock of blonde hair fell over her eyes. She pushed it back with a wrist, then said, "You know what she said?"

"No, what?"

"She said that Esther looks exactly like your mother did."

Jeff took a glass and dried it slowly. He was very thoughtful for a while. "You know, I guess one way to look at it is, as long as we've got Esther we've still got Ma, in a way."

"I guess that's right." Leah looked at him, surprised by the thought. "I never thought of it like that, but that's right, isn't it? Some of my ma and pa is in me, and when I grow up and get married and have babies, some of me will be in them. What a nice thing to say, Jeff!"

Jeff flushed as he always did when she paid him a compliment. He hastily dried the last dish. "Well, that's all of these. Why don't we go down and fish for a while?"

They told Silas their plans, and he agreed to them. So they went out toward the creek and, in doing so, had to pass by the barn.

Jeff said carelessly, "Not much need for a barn until you get your cow." He looked at the barn. "What's in there now?"

"Oh, nothing!" Leah said quickly. "Come on, Jeff." She took his arm and pulled him along.

"Hey! What's the hurry?" he protested. "Those fish'll wait until we get there."

Leah had suddenly thought what a horrible thing it would have been had Jeff stepped inside and come face to face with an enemy soldier. "Oh, I'm just anxious to fish," she said.

"Me too, but not as anxious as you." Jeff looked at her as she tugged him rapidly along. "Well, if we're gonna run, let's run. I'll race you."

"Good." Leah at once started running. Jeff, of course, caught up and easily passed her. He was waiting for her at the small creek when she got there, her cheeks red from the exercise.

"Well, I beat you at a footrace. Now I'm gonna beat you at catching fish," he said. "Let me have some of those worms."

The fish were small, but they bit at almost anything. Though Leah and Jeff released more than they kept, finally they had enough so that she said, "This will be fine, Jeff. You can stay for supper, can't you?"

"Oh, I sure can. If you can put me in a bunk somewhere, I'll stay the night."

Leah was suddenly apprehensive. She'd thought Jeff was going back to camp. *I've got to get out to take some food to Ezra*, she said to herself. But there was nothing to be done about it, so aloud she said, "Well, let's get the fish cleaned."

The rest of the afternoon they cleaned fish, and then Jeff sat on the porch and talked to Silas. Once he said, "You know, Mr. Carter, Leah seems a little bit nervous, don't you think?"

Silas bit his lip thoughtfully and raked his fingers through his beard. "Well, she has been kind of tetchy lately. Doesn't seem to be sleeping good. You don't think she's sick, do you?"

"She doesn't *look* sick," Jeff said. "Matter of fact, she looks better than I've ever seen her."

Silas Carter smiled at the boy. "She's a right pretty young woman—and that sister of hers, she is too." He peered at Jeff. "Your brother—Tom—he still hear from her?"

"Oh, yes, sir, real often."

"I guess they were pretty serious, weren't they?"

"Well, Tom wanted to marry her, but then the war came along, and we came South. The Carters —well, they're not sympathetic to the Confederacy. Of course, you know Sarah and Leah have got a brother in the Union army. I guess she was worried that he might kill Tom or Tom might kill him."

"I know. It's a brother's war, ain't it, boy? People that you'd be a good friend to, now you have to shoot at 'em. A shame."

The two talked quietly for a while longer, and then Leah came out. "I've fixed a place for you in the living room, Jeff," she said. "You can sleep on the couch."

"Be better than that broken-down cot I've got at camp." Jeff grinned. "How about some checkers?"

"All right."

Leah was an excellent checker player. Ordinarily she beat Jeff quite easily, but somehow her mind was elsewhere tonight.

"Why, I beat you three games out of four! What's wrong with you, Leah?" he finally asked. "Are you feeling bad? You look kind of flustered."

"Oh, I don't know. I'm all right," Leah said.

She lifted a hand and pushed a strand of hair back off her forehead so nervously that Jeff said, "Why are you so nervous, Leah?"

"I'm not!" she protested. "I'm not nervous at all."

Jeff leaned over and put his elbows on the table and stared at her. "Well, you're sure giving a good imitation of somebody who's nervous."

Leah forced herself to smile at him. "Let's play another game." She managed to beat him thoroughly this time and then said, "I expect we'd better get to bed. I have to get up early in the morning and make that pie for your father."

She waited until almost midnight. Then she got up, pulled on her robe and shoes, and carefully opened her door. In the kitchen she took out the pot of beans that was in the warmer of the oven, then gathered up several slices of bread and a big slice of the pie that she had made for Jeff.

She made her way out of the kitchen, across the moonlit yard, and noticed that Peanuts was coming with her, purring and pushing against her ankles. She pushed him away with her foot, then made for the barn.

Opening the door, she whispered, "Ezra!"

"Yes, I'm right here."

She stepped inside, leaving the door open. She saw that he had come down the stairs and was standing in the shadows. She handed him the food, saying, "How do you feel?"

"Feel some better. Fever broke sometime this afternoon. I got all sweaty, but I feel a lot better now."

"Are you hungry?"

"I sure am. I could eat anything."

"Well, come on and sit down. I can't stay long."

Ezra sat down near the open door and took the cover off the food. "Can't see too well, but, my, that smells good." He began to eat ravenously, cramming the food into his mouth and swallowing it as if he were starving. He looked up once and said, "My manners aren't very good, but I sure am hungry!"

"That's a good sign." Leah smiled at him. "That means you're getting better."

He finished the beans and the bread, licked his fingers, then picked up the piece of pie.

"I didn't have time to get a plate or a fork," she apologized.

"Pies are made to be et by hand," Ezra said. He took a bite. "That's the best pie I ever had in my whole life. You sure are a good cook, Leah."

"What part of the country do you come from? You haven't told me much about yourself, Ezra."

"Well—" he chewed thoughtfully on a bite of pie "—never had any folks," he said simply.

"Never had any folks! What do you mean?"

"Well—" he looked embarrassed "—I never knew who my father was—and my ma, she died when I was born."

"Oh, that's too bad," Leah said. "I'm so sorry. Who raised you?"

"I grew up in an orphanage until I was ten, then I got farmed out to a family. They lived on a farm. This was in Michigan, and I stayed there for about a year."

"Were they nice to you?"

"Well, not too nice," he said. He took another bite of pie. "I guess they mostly needed a boy to help, so they worked me pretty hard."

"But you only stayed a year?"

"Yeah, I run off," he said. "They caught me, of course, and brought me back. But they were so mad they took me back to the orphanage."

"What did you do then?"

"Oh, the next few years I kinda swapped around from one place to another, mostly on farms. Then when the war started, I'd had about all I could take of the last place. Old man Hiller, he was too handy with his strap, so I took off and I enlisted."

Leah stared at him. He didn't look a day over fifteen. He was not large, and his face was very thin. "How old are you, Ezra?"

"Sixteen now."

"You mean, the North took fifteen-year-old boys?"

"Oh, no. I had to fib about that a little." He smiled at her and ate the last bit of pie. Then he licked his fingers and wiped his hands on his shirt. "You know what we did to keep from lying when we went in the army when we were too young?"

"What did you do?"

"Well, you had to be eighteen to get in, so I took a sheet of paper and made two pieces of it. On each piece I wrote the figure eighteen, then I put them in my shoes."

Leah eyed him. "Why did you do that?"

Ezra smiled. He had nice brown eyes and was not a bad-looking boy. "When the recruiting sergeant asked me how old I was, I said, "Oh, I'm over eighteen."

Leah stared, then giggled, holding her hand over her mouth. "I never heard of anything like that."

Ezra nodded. "Lots of us did that. There was some men no more than fourteen, I'd guess. Big for their age, you know." He sat back and studied her. The moonlight flooded over her hair and gleamed in her eyes. "I liked the army," he said simply. "Course I wasn't in long before I got captured, but up until then it was the best I ever had."

"I'm sorry you got caught," she said, "but maybe the Lord did it that way on purpose."

Ezra blinked in surprise. "What does that mean?"

"I mean, if you hadn't gotten captured, maybe you'd have gotten killed. This last battle, there were thousands of men killed on both sides. Maybe God got you captured so you wouldn't get killed."

"I don't know anything about that—about God," Ezra said quietly. "They never told me nothing at any of the places where I was, except at the orphanage, and that was a long time ago."

Leah said, "I'm sorry about that. Everybody ought to get to hear about Jesus." A thought came to her then, and she said, "Would you mind if I would bring you a Bible? You could read it for yourself."

Ezra made a small face. "Well, I don't read too good, but I'll try if you want me to." He looked at her, and his face suddenly grew sober. "You've been awfully nice to me, Leah. Most Confederates would have had me hauled off right away."

Leah said quickly, "Well, I guess I'm not a real Confederate. I mean, we live in Kentucky, and that's kind of a border state. It's not on either side."

"But your pa, he works for the Union army, don't he?"

"Not exactly," Leah said. "He's a sutler. He follows the army and sells things to the soldiers: shaving soap, letter paper and pens and things like that. And he gives lots of Bibles away and tracts."

"Tracts? What's a tract?"

Leah thought, *He doesn't know anything!* Aloud she said, "It's just a little writing telling something about God and about the Christian life. I think Uncle Silas has some. I'll bring you one when I bring the Bible." Then she stood up. "I've got to go now. I'm glad you're better."

Young Ezra Payne stood up with her. "I sure am grateful for your help," he said. He reached out his hand suddenly and said, "I'd like to shake your hand."

Leah put her hand out slowly, and he grasped it.

His hand felt no larger than her own, he was so thin. But he pressed hers warmly.

"Good night, Ezra. I'll see you tomorrow. Be sure you stay out of sight. There's a young Confederate soldier staying with us tonight. I wouldn't want him to see you."

"A friend of yours?"

"Yes, I've known him a long time. His name's Jeff Majors. We grew up together. He comes by sometimes to check on me and my uncle."

"He's a lucky fellow."

"What do you mean?"

"Why, I mean getting to grow up in a nice place, around a nice girl like you." A longing came into the young man's eyes, and he shook his head. "I guess that must be pretty nice."

"Good night, Ezra. I'll see you tomorrow."

Leah slipped out of the barn and headed for the house. *I'll have to get a Bible,* she thought, *and some tracts. And he sure doesn't need to see Jeff!*

7
A Southern Belle

A knock at the door startled Leah.

"Who can that be, I wonder?" she asked Uncle Silas. When she passed into the front room, she saw a rather fat young man standing on the porch. "Yes? What is it?" she asked.

"Your name Carter?"

"Yes, I'm Leah Carter. I live here with my uncle Mr. Silas Carter."

The boy had a loose mouth, and he gave her a lazy grin. "I reckon this is for you then."

Leah opened the screen door and took the envelope the young man handed her. He was around sixteen. He had a moon face with dirty brown hair that fell over his ears and a pair of muddy brown eyes.

"I see the haints ain't got you yet."

Leah was accustomed to people referring to the so-called haunted house she and her uncle lived in. "Thank you for the note," she said stiffly.

"Oh, I better wait. You might want to send an answer."

"Very well." She closed the screen and went back to where Uncle Silas was waiting in the living room. "It's a note addressed to you." She stood watching while he opened it and saw his eyebrows go up.

"Well, I guess I'm going up in the world. This is a note from the Driscolls. They're wealthy planters who live about three miles down the road at Briarwood Plantation. They're having a party, and they want us to come."

"A *party!*" Leah said raising her eyebrows. "With a war going on!"

Uncle Silas shook his head and smiled faintly. "I guess they'd have a party if the world was coming to an end tomorrow. The Driscolls are pretty fancy folks. We can't go, of course." Then, "Wait a minute, I've got an idee. Why don't you and Jeff go to that party? She says here in the note she's especially interested in young people coming. She's heard about you, I take it."

"Oh, I couldn't go, Uncle Silas. I wouldn't know a soul. And anyway I'm not sure Jeff would be able to go."

"Well, we'll find out. Let me write a note to him. Is that boy outside the one who works for the Driscolls?"

"He didn't say."

"I expect it is. His name is Rufus Prather." He shook his head, adding, "He's the laziest human being I ever saw in my life. I guess he can take a note out to the camp for a dollar, though. Get the paper, will you, and pen and ink, and I'll write to Jeff."

A few minutes later Leah walked back to the door. "Is your name Rufus Prather?"

"Shore is. You can just call me Rufus, though." He grinned and rolled his eyes. "Always glad to have another pretty girl to come to settle around here."

Ignoring this, Leah gave him an envelope and a dollar. "My uncle wants to know if you'll take this to the camp and see that it gets to Private Jeff Majors."

"For a dollar? Well, I guess I will." The boy took the dollar and the letter and stuck them into his shirt pocket. "I'll be seeing you around, missy. We got to get better acquainted."

Leah peered at her choice of dresses, which amounted to two, her everyday dress and the "Sunday" dress she had brought with her. It was a high-waisted checkered gingham with a ruffle at the hem. It wasn't much of a party dress, but it was all that she had. She put it on, then sat down before the mirror and brushed her hair.

Leah never considered herself pretty. She was too tall and gawky, to her thinking. She had always admired petite girls, small ones who had to look up at men.

I don't look up at many. Then she smiled and said aloud, "Except for Jeff. I hope he keeps on growing. It's nice for a man to be tall like that." She ran the tortoise comb through her hair, which fell in honey-colored waves almost down to her waist. Finally she braided it and put it in a coil on the back of her head.

When she heard a horse and buggy pulling up on the road, she reached into a drawer and drew out her only piece of jewelry. Carefully she removed the gold locket and held it for a moment. She opened it and smiled at the image of Jeff peering straight at her, unsmiling. *He has such a nice smile,* she thought. *I don't know why he's scowling like he's got to pick cotton.* She snapped the chain to fasten it behind her neck, then walked to the door.

Jeff was just mounting the steps. "Oh! Well, you're all ready. That's a shock!"

Leah saw that he was wearing his dress uniform with two rows of small buttons down the front. It was ash gray, and he had a campaign hat pulled down over his eyes. He'd gotten that trick, she knew, from Stonewall Jackson.

"I'm never late," she said. "I'm ready if you are. Let me say good night to Uncle Silas."

Soon the two were on their way, and Jeff said, "I wish we had a fancy buggy, but this wagon's all I could commandeer. And these mules may be fit for plowing, but they're not very stylish."

"As long as they get us there, Jeff, that's all right. Tell me what you've been doing." She sat jolting along on the rough road and listening as he rambled on about what had been happening in the camp.

Then she said, "I don't know any of these people, the Driscolls. I wish Uncle Silas could have gone with us."

"Well, we're even. They don't know us either." Jeff grinned. He had pulled his cap off, and his black hair was slightly curly from having just been washed.

A thought came to her. "Jeff, I hope you never grow whiskers."

"*Whiskers!* What made you think of a thing like that?"

"Oh, I don't know. Uncle Silas looks nice with his. Old men with white beards sort of look like Santa Claus, but I think most beards are just foolish. Don't raise any whiskers, please."

He laughed at her. "Won't promise that. Stonewall's got whiskers, and so has General Lee. That's good enough for me!"

The two of them continued to enjoy each other's company, and at last they arrived at a very large two-story house set back off the road. Eight huge pillars in front formed a portico, and the windows on the first floor blazed with light. They could hear the sound of music—fiddles and what sounded like a banjo.

"Guess they've already started," Jeff said.

He pulled up the mules in front of the house, and a servant came to say, "Take these mules, suh?"

"Yes, thanks." Jeff looked at the fancy carriages and thoroughbred horses that were tied to a rail farther down, and he grinned at the man. "I guess these would do better to plow than to come to a place like this."

"Fine-looking animals, Captain." The man grinned back, his teeth white in his black face. "I'll take good care of 'em for you."

"That was a quick promotion," Jeff murmured. "Captain in one moment. Well, let's get inside."

They mounted the steps and were met at the door by a tall, distinguished-looking man. He had a full beard, brown and well-tended, and he smiled, saying, "We haven't met. I'm John Driscoll, and this is my wife, Edith."

"You must know my Uncle Silas," Leah said. "I'm Leah Carter, and this is Jeff Majors."

"Oh, yes." Mr. Driscoll nodded. "I've heard about you. Good to have you with us, Miss Carter, and you too, Private. What's your unit?"

"Stonewall Brigade," Jeff said proudly.

"Well now, that makes you doubly welcome. Any member of that brigade is a hero in our eyes. Come along. I'll take you to where the young people are."

They passed out of the large foyer and turned to the right into what was one of the largest rooms Leah had ever seen in a private house. Candles and chandeliers threw brilliant light over the floor, and tables along the walls were set with crystal glasses and shiny china plates loaded with food.

The two followed Mr. Driscoll to the end of the room where a group of young people was chattering. "I hate to interrupt, but you have two new guests. This is my daughter, Lucy," Mr. Driscoll said. "Lucy, this is Miss Leah Carter, Silas Carter's niece, and this is her escort, Private Jeff Majors." He smiled broadly and said, "Of the Stonewall Brigade. I'm sure you will welcome them."

Lucy Driscoll looked at Leah. "So good to have you, Leah." But then she turned to Jeff and smiled brilliantly. "Private Majors, how *nice* to have you!"

Lucy was a small girl, well-shaped and possessing that prettiness that Leah always envied. She had curly blonde hair, light blue eyes, and a rosebud mouth. She was approximately Leah's age but somehow behaved as if she were much older.

"You must tell us about your campaigns with General Jackson," Lucy said. "First, let me make introductions." She introduced them to the group, some seven or eight young people, and then said, "Now, come. We'll have some refreshments. Cecil, why don't you escort Miss Leah? I want to hear what this young soldier has to say."

A thin young man with chestnut hair and a pair of bright blue eyes said, "Come along, if you will, Miss Carter. You won't be seeing much of your escort anymore."

Leah glanced at him with surprise. "Why, whatever do you mean?"

"Didn't you see how Lucy took him right off? She's that way, our Lucy is. Pretty as a picture, but sometimes she does show unseemly interest in new young men."

Cecil was correct. For the next two hours, Lucy did not let Jeff out of her sight. She smiled at him and touched his arm as she leaned forward to give a tinkling laugh from time to time.

As for Jeff, Leah saw that he was enjoying himself immensely. She had always thought him a rather shy boy, but he seemed to blossom under Lucy's constant attention. *He's making a fool out of himself,* she thought shortly. *You'd think he'd never seen a girl before in his whole life!*

She herself was not having a good time. All the other girls were wearing dresses of silk and satin and fine cloth. They were bedecked with bows. Most wore jewelry and had had their hair dressed, it seemed, by experts. Leah felt like a clod, wearing her old checkered dress. *I wish I could get out of here,* she thought grimly. *I feel like an old donkey in with all these other girls.*

Cecil was a good host, however, and saw to it she had plenty of refreshments. When Lucy dragged Jeff to the dance floor and he was not *too* reluctant, Cecil said, "May I have this dance, Miss Leah?"

"Well, I don't dance very well."

"Well, I dance superbly," he said with a grin.

He was not tall, so she looked him right in the eye as they went out on the floor. She found he had not misled her; he was a beautiful dancer.

"I haven't had much practice," she said.

"You're doing splendidly." Cecil nodded. "What do you think of this house? Fine, isn't it?"

"Beautiful. I've never been in a mansion like this."

Her honesty caused Cecil to blink in surprise. "Most young ladies would not have admitted such a thing."

He studied Leah as they moved about the floor, and he must have noticed that she kept looking around for Jeff.

The evening wore on, and Leah grew more comfortable. The young people drew away into a large parlor and played games for a while. They talked of the war, and Jeff spoke somewhat boastfully of what the Stonewall Brigade was going to do in the future.

Suddenly Lucy turned and fixed her eyes on Leah. "You're not from around here, are you, Leah?"

"No, I'm from Kentucky."

Lucy's eyebrows went up. "Kentucky? That's one of the border states, isn't it?"

"Yes, it is."

"Which side are your people for, the North or the Confederacy?"

A silence fell over the room, and Leah felt her cheeks redden. She understood clearly that the question was not accidental. Lucy Driscoll was, she had found out, an ardent supporter of the South. Cecil had told her that much. Now she knew that she was being put on some sort of trial.

It would have been simple to have lied, but she said quietly, "I have a brother in the Federal army, and my father serves as a sutler for that same army."

Lucy blinked at Leah's bluntness. She glanced at Jeff, who seemed embarrassed, then shook her head. "I wouldn't think you would be very comfortable here in the Confederacy with attachments like that," she said smoothly.

Cecil spoke up instantly. "Oh, come on, Lucy. Let's don't talk politics. This is a *party*."

Leah gave him a grateful glance. But the evening was spoiled for her, and she was glad when finally nine o'clock came and she was able to say, "Jeff, I think I'd better get home."

Jeff was talking, as usual, with Lucy, and he turned to her reluctantly. "Why, it's early yet!"

Lucy said, "We can have one of the servants take Leah home if you'd like to stay longer, Jeff."

For one moment Leah thought that Jeff meant to take advantage of Lucy Driscoll's offer. It must have shown in her face, for he said hurriedly, "Oh, no, I couldn't do that, Miss Lucy. We sure have had a fine time, haven't we, Leah?"

"It's been very nice," Leah said.

"Oh, we must do this again." Lucy gave her hand to Jeff, who shook it. Then she turned and examined Leah carefully. "I hope you haven't been embarrassed being around so many who are dedicated to the Confederate cause."

Leah did not know how to answer and merely said, "Thank you. It was kind of your parents to ask us."

They left in the wagon, and Jeff talked excitedly for the first mile. Then he must have noticed that Leah was saying almost nothing. "What's the matter?"

"Nothing," she said quickly.

He turned to look at her in the moonlight. "You didn't get your feelings hurt, did you? Lucy didn't mean anything by what she said."

"I'm all right."

But later, when Jeff told Tom about the evening, explaining how Lucy had mentioned that Leah was not a Confederate, his brother stared at him. "No wonder she was depressed. Who wouldn't be?" he said in exasperation.

"What do you mean?" Jeff asked, bewildered.

Tom gave his younger brother a look and shook his head. "If you don't know, I can't tell you."

8
Jeff Gets a Shock

For two days Jeff mooned around camp until finally his father demanded, "What's the matter with you, son? You act like you're sick. Don't you feel well?"

"Oh, I feel all right. I just—well, I don't think I was too nice to Leah when I took her to the party."

Captain Majors stared at him. He had sharp hazel eyes and a black mustache and the same jet black hair he'd passed on to his sons. "You want to tell me about it? We haven't had a father-and-son talk in quite a while."

Jeff looked embarrassed. He examined his boots silently for a while, then nodded. He began to relate the events that had taken place, and when he got to the part that embarrassed him most, his cheeks reddened. He ended by saying, "I know Leah felt pretty bad. She was ashamed of her dress, but that didn't bother me. What bothers me is I left her alone so much."

"This girl—the daughter of the house, Lucy— was she pretty?"

Jeff swallowed, then nodded. "Yes, sir, she was." He cracked his knuckles nervously. "I just made a mess out of it, Pa. After all the Carters have done for me, you'd think I had better sense."

Nelson Majors put a hand on his son's shoulder. "When I was your age," he said gently, "I was in something like this all the time. My pa used to tell me I was studying for the gallows. You know what I think you better do?"

"What's that?"

"I think you better have another quick leave and go tell that girl how sorry you are. Take her something nice—a present of some kind. I know what—take her some coffee. I managed to get a couple of pounds. Take some of it to her for her uncle. He likes it so much."

"Yes, sir!" Jeff exclaimed. "I'll be back as soon as I can. And thanks a lot, sir."

Jeff managed to catch a ride from the camp out to Richmond Manor. He knew he would probably have to walk back, so he wouldn't have long to stay.

He walked up onto the porch, knocked loudly, and heard a voice say, "Come in!"

He stepped inside, looking for Leah. He didn't see her, but then Silas Carter called, "Come on in the living room."

Jeff proceeded into the front room and saw that the old man was sitting in his rocking chair reading his Bible.

"Why, hello, Jeff! Didn't expect to see you today."

Jeff was embarrassed. "Well, I just had a chance to come for a minute. Is Leah around?"

"She's outside, hunting eggs. You know how it is with guineas, don't you? We got half a dozen of them from a neighbor. They make good eating, and their eggs are good too, but they hide those things like nothing you ever saw. Keeps Leah busy hunting for them. But you'll find her out there somewhere."

"Yes, sir. I'll go look for her."

Jeff stood on the porch and scanned the terrain, but he didn't see her. He circled the house, looking out into the field and finally muttering to himself, "She's got to be here somewhere. Those guineas wouldn't stray over into the woods—too many critters there to eat them up." He began to walk in a circle, expecting to see her any minute.

Then Jeff came to the area where the small barn sat back from the house. *Maybe she's behind the barn.* As he passed the barn door, which was standing ajar, he heard a voice.

"That's probably her, calling those guineas," he said. He stepped up to the door, and the voice grew louder.

That's not Leah, he thought, puzzled. *Must be one of the neighbors with her.* He pulled the door open and stepped inside. "Leah! I came out to—"

Jeff halted abruptly, for there to Leah's right was a young man in a tattered Federal uniform. He stood dumbfounded, staring at the pair, not believing his eyes. Then his mind worked quickly. "Who are you, and what are you doing here?" he demanded.

Leah gave him a frightened look and took two steps toward him. "Jeff, I can explain."

"You can't explain an enemy soldier in your barn," Jeff said. He wished he'd brought a musket with him. He examined the soldier carefully but saw no sign of a weapon. "You must be an escaped prisoner."

"He is, Jeff. This is Ezra Payne."

Jeff took a cautious step forward, his hands doubling up into fists. The soldier was not large. His eyes were sunk in his head, and he looked almost fragile. *I can take him back,* Jeff thought confidently. *He doesn't look like he'd put up much of a struggle.* "Leah, don't you worry," Jeff said confidently. "I'll see to it that he gets returned."

"No, Jeff, you can't do that!" Leah turned to the young soldier and put her hand on his arm. "Don't you see—he's sick!"

Jeff stared at the boy. He did look sick and very young. "How long have you been here?"

Ezra Payne shook his head. "Not too long. This young lady—it's not her fault." Apparently he could see trouble ahead and didn't want Leah to get involved with his problem.

But Leah's lips closed firmly, and she turned to face Jeff. "Yes, it *is* my fault. He's been here for several days, Jeff. When I found him, he was almost dead. He's still sick."

Jeff stared at her. "Well, I'm sorry about that, but he's got to go back to prison, Leah. Maybe the doctors at the hospital—"

"You know they don't even have time to take care of the Confederate wounded. The hospitals are filled. They're not going to pay any attention to one Union boy with fever."

Jeff was disturbed by the determined look on Leah's face. He knew she was stubborn and could see she had made up her mind to help this Yankee.

"Leah," he said, "do you know you could be put in prison for doing a thing like this? It's against the law to hide escaped enemy soldiers."

"I know that!"

"Well, you'll just have to let me take him back then. Come on, Payne. You'll have to go back."

The Northern soldier shrugged and stepped forward, but Leah grabbed his arm. Then she fixed her eyes on Jeff. "Jeff! He's going to go back, but he nearly died in Belle Isle. He was there for almost a year. If he'd gone back as sick as he was, he wouldn't have lasted a week. He's still too sick. As soon as he's well, he'll go back."

"How do you know that?" Jeff demanded. "As soon as he's well, he'll run away, and in the meantime—if anybody saw him here—you know what would happen."

"I don't care!" Leah exclaimed. "He's too sick to go back yet."

"Just imagine what would happen if Captain Lyons found out about this. He's still sore about what happened with Sarah and you. He still thinks you're both spies." He hesitated and then said angrily, "And it's almost true. After all, he *is* an enemy soldier."

Leah did not give ground. "He's just a sick boy right now. When he gets well, then he can go back."

Jeff glared at her angrily. Then he said something he should not have said. "Maybe Lucy's right about you being a Yankee."

"Jeff! You know that's not so!"

"All I know is, here's a Yankee soldier, and you're keeping him from being taken." He shook his head and added, "You're always taking everything that's sick, every kind of critter that ever came to your place—but this isn't an animal that you're taking in. This is an enemy soldier, a member of the Yankee army. I just can't let you do it, Leah!"

Leah said slowly, "Jeff, I'm going to take care of him for now, and then he'll go back to prison. He's promised me that, and I believe he'll keep his word. If you want to turn us in, you'll just have to do it, but I'm going to do exactly what I said."

Jeff Majors stared at the girl. She was standing straight and tall, her blonde hair tied back and her blue-green eyes looking at him boldly. He knew that she meant exactly what she said. Finally he shrugged. "You know I won't turn you in—but somebody else probably will. Have you thought then what'll happen to your uncle? He's sick too, and he'll go to jail along with you."

Leah had no answer for that, and indeed she hadn't thought of it. Now she saw that Jeff himself was in a terrible position. Her voice softened, and she said, "I'm sorry, Jeff. I know you're a soldier in the Confederate Army—and ordinarily if he was strong and well I wouldn't say a word, but I just can't do it, Jeff. I can't!"

Jeff Majors stood silent, knowing there was nothing he could do. Then he remembered the small package of coffee in his hand. He looked down at it and said, "I brought you some coffee." He held it out.

She took it and started to speak, but he interrupted.

"I've got to go back to camp. Good-bye." He turned and left abruptly without saying another word.

Leah watched him go and had seldom felt as bad in her whole life.

Ezra was watching her. "You should have let him take me," he said quietly. "I ought to have gone anyhow. I don't want you to get in any trouble on account of me, Leah."

"No, you've got to stay here. Jeff was telling the truth—he won't tell. Pretty soon you'll be strong enough. Then maybe he'll understand."

Ezra looked around the barn, glancing up the steps to where he had made a little room for himself. He had a bed—at least a cot—and blankets and a wash pan. He turned to face her and said, "You know what, Leah?" When she looked at him, he smiled. "This is the best home I ever had—and you're the best friend I ever had."

"Oh, Ezra—"

"It's true. Whatever happens from now on, I'll never forget you, Leah, and not ever!"

9

A Noble Deed

From the time she rose early in the morning, Leah found herself tense and unable to concentrate. She fixed breakfast, but after she had sat at the table for a while, Silas asked, "What's the matter? You're not eating anything, Leah."

"Oh," she said, looking down at her plate. She realized she had been staring at her food, thinking about Ezra out in the barn—and about Jeff and what he was doing. "I guess I'm not very hungry."

"As hard as you hunted for those guinea eggs, you'd better eat them," Uncle Silas said. He looked at her carefully. "You've got circles under your eyes," he commented. "Didn't you sleep good last night?"

"Not very well," she admitted.

"You're not still thinking this is a haunted house, are you? I think you've got more judgment than that."

"Oh, no, it's nothing like that, Uncle Silas." Leah took a huge mouthful of scrambled eggs so that she wouldn't have to answer for a while. She forced herself to eat, then afterward washed the dishes and began cleaning the little house.

As she worked, she thought about Jeff. *He's my best friend. The best friend I've ever had. I know he wouldn't turn me in. But it's bound to be hard on him, just knowing what's going on.*

Later that day she found an excuse to go to the barn. She'd almost reached it when a voice said, "Well, hello there, Leah."

Startled, she turned around to see Rufus Prather, who evidently had been walking by on the road.

He came now to where she stood, grinning. "I heard you went to the big party over at our place. Wish I could have gone, but I guess they're not about to ask their hired help to their play parties." He was wearing a pair of old overalls, stiff with dirt, and had a straw hat shoved back on his head. "How about I come over and sit on the porch with you a little bit?"

"Oh, no, I don't think so," Leah said quickly. "Uncle Silas doesn't need any visitors right now. He's not well, you know."

Rufus reached out and squeezed her arm. "You're a right pretty gal," he said. "Maybe you and me could take a walk sometime. Maybe even go to Richmond."

Leah was half frightened of the boy. He was large and, though fat, seemed extremely strong. She'd heard how lazy he was, but there was also something she didn't like about his muddy brown eyes. "I don't go to town much," she said.

She turned and walked back to the house, ignoring his promise to come to see her anyway. She found herself trembling, for if he had seen her go into the barn, he might have followed her.

All day long she kept well away from the barn. Uncle Silas slept, as usual, most of the afternoon, and she contented herself with reading a book called *The Last of the Mohicans*, by a man named Cooper.

Ordinarily she liked adventures, but she could hardly keep her mind on what she was reading.

Finally suppertime came, and Uncle Silas seemed to feel so much better that he stayed up very late. He talked a great deal about his youthful days when he had been a salesman on the road. She was glad to see him feeling better, but she was anxious to get out and see how Ezra was.

At last her uncle yawned and said, "Well, Leah, this is the latest I've stayed up in a spell. I think I'll get to bed now."

"Good night, Uncle Silas."

"Good night. You sleep well tonight now. If you feel you're coming down with some kind of the flu, you better get you a toddy or some kind of medicine."

"Oh, no, I'm all right! You go to bed." She went over and kissed him on the cheek, and he smiled and patted her shoulder.

"You're a fine girl, Leah, you and that sister of yours both."

Leah waited for more than an hour until she was absolutely certain that he was asleep. She even stood in front of his door, listening to his deep, regular breathing. Then she gathered up some food and a candle and left for the barn.

Stepping inside, she called out, "Ezra?"

But there was no answer.

At once Leah knew something was wrong. "Ezra!" she called out more loudly. She lifted the candle, walked up the stairs to where his cot was, and saw a note on the bed. It was by the Bible she had given him to read.

Quickly she seized it and saw printed in large crudely made letters, "Leah, I thank you for all your goodness. I have never known anyone like you. It's not good for me to stay here anymore. I might get you and your uncle in trouble. I will never forget you. Good-bye." It was signed, "Ezra Payne."

Leah put the food on the cot and went down the steps. *He can't make it! He'll be caught before morning,* she thought. *I'll have to find him.*

She blew out the candle and stood at the barn door trying to decide which way to look. Then she recalled telling Ezra that there was a path alongside the creek that followed the road. She had told him furthermore that you could walk along that path a long way toward the North-South border and never be seen.

Still, he might have gone any number of ways. She continued to stand there uncertainly, the darkness closing about her. She suddenly said out loud, "Lord, help me to find him, if that's what You want."

Then she ran toward the stream.

The moonlight was bright enough to enable her to see her way. She moved quickly along the path, and not more than ten minutes later she saw a form ahead outlined like a shadow. She stopped abruptly. "Ezra? Is that you?"

"Yes, it's me."

Leah hurried to where he stood. He had left behind the clothes that belonged to Uncle Silas, and she knew immediately he had done that in case he got caught. He was again wearing only the thin shirt and pants he had worn when she first saw him, not even a hat on his head.

"You shouldn't have run away, Ezra," she said. "You're not strong enough yet."

Somewhere far off a dog barked furiously. They listened until the sound died away.

Then Ezra shook his head. "I couldn't let you take any more chances on my account," he said simply. "I couldn't bear it if anything happened to you, Leah."

She took a deep breath and sighed. "Come on, Ezra. Nothing's going to happen. Another week and you'll be strong enough." She took his arm and pulled at him, and he surrendered.

They'd gone halfway back to the barn when he said, "I'm afraid I've got to rest a little bit. Guess I'm not as strong as I thought."

"Look—sit on that log over there."

They both sat down on a fallen tree trunk, and she heard his breath coming in a raspy wheeze. "You've got some kind of sickness, Ezra. You're still not well. I'm going to town tomorrow and find a doctor and get some medicine."

"No, don't do that!" he said in alarm. "I'll be all right. Just give me a little time."

Leah made up her mind, however, though she did not pursue the matter. The stream flowed by over to their left. The moon made a huge silver reflection that was broken as a fish broke the surface with a loud splash.

"I'd like to come here and catch you," Leah said to the fish.

"I never went fishing. Is it fun?"

"You never went *fishing?* I think that's awful!"

"Well, I was mostly working, and they didn't fish much where I came from." He hesitated, then said, "I've been reading the Bible you left."

"Have you, Ezra? Do you like it?"

92

He hesitated. "Well, I'm not sure as I understand much of it, but what I do get is that God seems to love us. I never knew that. The sermons I heard was mostly about hell and how that God was gonna put us there if we didn't do good."

"Have you been reading in the book of John, like I said?"

"Yeah, sure have. That's a good one. You know, I never thought about Jesus being a man. I mean, He got tired, He went to sleep, He got hungry, just like me. I never thought about that," he said in a wondering tone.

"Yes, that's what He was—a man." Leah nodded. "While He was here on earth anyhow."

"But He was God too, wasn't He? How could He be God and still be like us?"

"I don't think I can explain it very well," Leah said, "but the preachers all say—and my father told me—that God wanted to save people and the only way He could do it was for Him to send His Son to die."

"I read that part—about where they nailed Him to a cross." Ezra shifted on the log and turned to face her. "That made me cry. I don't remember ever crying, not in a long time, but that did."

"It makes me cry too sometimes," Leah said, "to think that God's own Son would die for us."

The silence ran on, and finally Leah said, "Ezra, have you ever asked God to forgive your sins?"

"No, I never have."

"Would you like to do that right now?"

"You mean, right out here? You don't have to be in a church?"

"No, there weren't any churches like we have when Jesus was on earth. He often preached to people out on the road or on a hill or in a boat. It doesn't matter where you are. Anytime you call on God, He'll save you."

"Well, I sure need saving, I guess. Don't know why He'd want to do a thing like that for me."

"He does want to. He loves every one of us." Leah turned to Ezra and said, "Let's just pray. I'll pray out loud, and you just talk to God any way you can—in your own heart, if you want. You don't have to say a word out loud if you don't want to. Will you do that?"

After a long silence, he nodded. "Yes, Miss Leah, I sure will."

Leah prayed a short prayer, asking God to bless the young soldier. She asked Him to help Ezra see his need of trusting Christ, and, when she had finished the prayer, she asked, "Did you ask God?"

"Yes, I did." He looked at her and said, "Is that all there is to it?"

"No, there's lots more, but if you've asked Jesus into your heart, you've taken the first step. Now wherever you go, He'll go with you."

Ezra Payne sat on the log. He was sick and weak, had never known a home, and was far from the place of his birth, among enemies. He looked at the young girl, the kindest person he'd ever known, and then he said, "Well, Leah, I sure need somebody to be with me, because I've been alone all my life."

10

He Can Stay

Jeff went about his duties for the next two days, moody and sullen.

Tom threatened to stick his head under the pump if he didn't straighten up. "You're acting like a bear with a sore tail," he told him sternly. "We've got a war to fight here, and you're not helping any acting like a spoiled brat."

Jeff glared at him but made no answer, for he knew Tom was right. He was aware that there were stirrings in the camp. A battle might be in the offing, and he asked his father about it.

"There's a Federal general called Pope, who's taking charge of one of the Yankee armies. He's already made General Lee mad."

"General Lee got mad? What did Pope do?" Jeff demanded, amazed.

"Why, he said he was going to deal harshly with any Confederate sympathizers in the Shenandoah Valley. He's going to treat civilians like spies, maybe even have them shot."

"Why, he can't do that! Not civilians!"

Tom shook his head. "Not much telling what a general will do. General Lee said Pope must be stopped. They said he was about as mad as he ever gets." He looked over at the troops that were drilling out in the field. "We're sure whittled down thin, Jeff. We lost so many men at Seven Days that we're just not ready to fight a battle."

"Why, we can whip 'em, can't we, Tom?"

Tom ran his hand through his hair. There was a doubtful look in his eye. "We're outnumbered. Always will be," he murmured. "No matter how many men they lose, they've always got another man to put in his place. But every time we lose a man, it just leaves a gap. It's gonna be a tough thing, Jeff."

Jeff had never for one moment considered that the South might lose, and it troubled him.

Later that afternoon he was assigned with Charlie Bowers, a drummer-boy friend, to take a wagon into Richmond for supplies. Charlie was a cheerful, undersized young fellow of fourteen. He had tow-colored hair and bright blue eyes. Curly Henson, a big red-haired corporal, drove the wagon. He had been hard on Jeff at first but then had saved Jeff's life in a battle, and he had become fond of both boys.

They drove into the city, and the streets were filled with buggies and horses and men and women walking along busily. Richmond was the busiest town in the Confederacy. It was not only the heart of the government but the heart of a great deal of its industry.

When Curly pulled up in front of the warehouse, he said, "I can load this wagon. You fellows go to the store and try to find me some chewing tobacco." He gave them a dollar bill, adding, "Get yourself some candy, if you can find any."

The two of them grinned at the big man and left. As they were about to enter a store, Jeff stopped dead still, for Leah was coming out, a basket under her arm.

* * *

96

"Hello, Jeff."

"Why . . . hello, Leah." There was an awkward silence, and Jeff said, "Everything . . . all right?"

Leah knew immediately what he meant. "Oh, yes, everything's fine, Jeff." She looked at Charlie Bowers and knew she could not say much. "The problem we were talking about—it's going to be all right."

It appeared Jeff hardly knew what to say to her and felt awkward. Finally he said abruptly, "Well, we've got to go. Good-bye, Leah."

She was disappointed. She had hoped that Jeff would be more ready to listen. Back at Richmond Manor she was met by her uncle. He held out an envelope and said, "Another invitation."

"Invitation to what?" Leah asked.

"It's Lucy Driscoll's birthday. She sent a note especially for you."

Instantly Leah knew what had happened. "She didn't do it because she wanted to. I bet her parents made her send it."

"Oh, don't talk like that," Uncle Silas said, his face showing surprise. "I think you ought to go. Not much fun for a young girl like you around here."

"I don't want to, Uncle Silas."

"Is it because you don't have anything to wear? I know that you felt bad last time, but you could make a new dress, if that's what you want to do."

Leah felt tired and discouraged. The strain of the past days had worn on her. She hadn't slept well and was constantly expecting someone to stumble upon Ezra. "I'm just tired," she said. "And she doesn't really want me to come."

"Well, it's as you say." Silas nodded. "Write her a note then. That no-account Rufus Prather's been hanging around a lot. I expect he's sweet on you."

"I don't like him, Uncle Silas."

"He's a lazy, shiftless boy. I don't want him hanging around. I'll tell him so the next time, but he's handy for carrying letters. Write a note—we'll send it to the Driscolls."

"All right. I'll do that."

Leah found paper and pen and wrote a brief letter thanking the Driscolls for the invitation and using the excuse that her uncle still wasn't feeling well and she wouldn't feel comfortable leaving him.

Later that afternoon she saw Rufus Prather about to drive past in a wagon. She ran out to the road, and he pulled up at once.

"Why, howdy, Leah," he said. "Come on, we'll go for a ride."

"No, I can't do that. Would you give this note to Mr. or Mrs. Driscoll, Rufus?"

"Shore, I'll do that." Rufus stuck it carelessly into his pocket. "You coming to that birthday party, aren't you?"

"I don't think so."

Rufus nodded. "I don't blame you. They're too highfalutin, all those Driscolls. Now, me and you —we're alike."

Leah gave him a half-angry, half-amused look. He was such a stupid boy that it would be hard to explain how exactly they were *not* alike. She handed him the dollar that Uncle Silas had given her and said, "There! That's for delivering the note."

Later in the afternoon, Uncle Silas lay down to take a nap. After he had been asleep for some time, Leah thought it would be safe to go out and talk to Ezra. She closed the screen door very quietly. She had bought a half dozen apples and carried one with her.

When she got to the barn, she found him waiting for her.

"I was watching through the door and saw you coming," he said.

She held out the apple. "Here. I got a few of these in town. I ate one—they're real good."

Ezra took the apple, polished it on his sleeve, and nodded. "Thank you. Nothing I like better than a good apple. You eat half of it."

"No, I've already had one. You go ahead, Ezra."

They sat down in the hay, and Ezra ate the apple very slowly, enjoying it.

"You look better," she said. "Your face has got a little color in it."

"All that good food I've been getting." Ezra took another bite and chewed thoughtfully. "I figure it won't be long before I'll be off your hands."

Leah asked, "Have you been reading the Bible more?"

"Sure have. Still don't understand lots of it. But you know what? I feel good, Leah. Ever since we prayed, I feel like God's just doing something for me." A smile lighted his face.

He'd be really a nice-looking boy, Leah thought, *if he were well-fed.* He had clean features and unusually good teeth, bright and even. His eyes were alert now, and there was a restfulness about him that she had not seen before.

"I just feel like I've settled it all with God," he said. "You know, I saw some fellows do that when I first went in the army. Had a service there, and some of them went. They came back and said they'd gotten converted. I didn't even know what they were talking about." He looked down at his feet. "Two of them got killed at Bull Run. Sure hope they're all right."

"If they trusted in Jesus, they're all right," Leah said stoutly.

They sat talking, mostly about God. Then Ezra got the Bible and began to point out Scriptures and ask her what they meant. They were so deeply engrossed in what they were doing that both of them leaped to their feet when a voice said, "Leah! What's this?"

"Uncle Silas!"

Her uncle stood at the barn door. He had not been out-of-doors very much, and he was leaning heavily on a cane. His eyes were fixed on the young man with her.

"Uncle Silas, this is Ezra Payne," Leah said.

Silas Carter studied the boy and asked quietly, "Escaped prisoner, are you, boy?"

"Yes, sir. I was in Belle Isle ever since Bull Run." He said quickly, "Don't get mad at Miss Leah. I was about dead when she found me. If they'd taken me back, I'd have died for sure. I'm going back— I'm going to give myself up right away."

"He was so sick, Uncle Silas," Leah said, "but he's better now. Please, you won't give him away. I know you won't!"

"Well, I don't know. It's a serious thing to harbor an escaped prisoner," Silas said. "We could all be in terrible trouble."

"That's what I've told her, Mr. Carter," Ezra said.

"Yes, and he left once—he was trying to save us trouble—but he was so weak he couldn't do it." Leah went over and stood beside her uncle. She was almost as tall as he was. "I think the Lord is in it."

"The Lord? How do you mean that?"

"Ezra got saved. He didn't know anything about the Lord. We prayed together, and now he knows Jesus."

Uncle Silas looked at the boy and asked, "Is that right, son?"

"Yes, sir," Ezra said simply. "I never heard no preaching before, and I don't know much, but I know ever since I asked God to forgive me that things have been . . . well . . . *different* somehow."

Silas Carter was silent, perhaps thinking about the possible difficulties that could arise. He asked suddenly, "Does Jeff know about this?"

"Yes." Leah nodded.

"And he agreed not to tell, I suppose. That's hard on him."

"I know it is, but he won't tell, and it's just for a few more days, Uncle Silas."

Silas thought hard. Then he said, "Well, if a man's hurt and sick, I don't guess it matters if he wears the blue or the gray."

"You'll let him stay?" Leah asked, her eyes bright with hope.

"Until he gets well, he can stay."

Ezra dropped his head. He said nothing for a moment, and when he lifted his eyes they were brimming with tears. "I never met people like you before, but I'm sure glad I have. No matter what happens, things are gonna be different with me from now on."

11

A Friend Loves
at All Times

Jeff was awakened out of sound sleep by a rough hand on his shoulder.

"Get up, Jeff! The regiment's moving out—part of it anyway." Tom was already dressed.

Since becoming sergeant, Tom had been rough on his troops, and no less so on his own brother. At times Jeff thought Tom was even stricter on him than on anybody else. *I guess he's got to be*, he thought, *so he won't show favoritism.*

He rolled out of his blankets and pulled his clothes on. It had been a warm night, and the east was already glowing with the rising of the sun.

As Jeff put on his uniform, Sgt. Henry Mapes stopped by. He was tall and rangy, with black eyes and hair, and had seen considerable action. He had been a regular in the United States Army but left when his state seceded. "Don't forget your drums," he told the two boys, for Charlie Bowers too was dressing, even while blinking away sleep.

"Where we going, Sarge?" Jeff asked.

"We heard there was a breakthrough. Some of the Yankees coming in from the west—over by White Oaks Swamp bridge."

"Think it'll be a big battle?" Charlie asked. His eyes were dull with sleep, and he yawned hugely.

"It better be—to get me out of a sound sleep like I was having. I dreamed I was at the circus."

"Well, you might get a chance to see the elephant today, but I don't know what else."

That was what the soldiers on both sides called seeing action—"going to see the elephant."

Mapes hurried away, and soon the boys were beating a tattoo on their drums to rout out the sleeping troops. Then the men ate a hastily prepared breakfast and marched out with Charlie and Jeff at their head, right behind the staff officers.

"This won't be a big fight," Jeff said.

"How do you know?" Charlie asked.

"Because we're not carrying extra rations. If it was going to be a big struggle, we'd get three days' cooked rations. You know that, Charlie."

They left Richmond at a fast pace. Somewhere up ahead Jeff heard a cavalry troop thundering along the road, but it veered off to the west. They marched hard till noon, stopping only once to eat cold rations.

As the men sat around resting, Tom took out a sheet of paper and a pencil and began to scribble.

"Writin' to your girl, are you, Sarge?" Curly Henson teased. The big redhead winked at Jeff. "Tell us about her, Jeff. Is she as pretty as that little gal I seen you with in town?"

Jeff glanced at Tom, not knowing if he could take teasing or not, but Tom paid no heed. "It's her sister, Sarah."

"Why, that's a right pretty name." Henson nodded. "I had a gal named Sarah once. Law, she was as pretty as a pair of red shoes with green strings. I sure would like to be going to a pie supper with my Sarah today."

103

"You won't be going to a pie supper, I don't reckon," Tom looked up to say. "If we bump into Pope's boys, it'll be a right smart skirmish."

Henson shrugged. He was not a man who thought a great deal, and he returned to his former subject. "What about these two gals? How come you can get gals and the rest of us can't?"

Jeff bit off some hardtack. It was tough and hard, but he managed to get it down. "We've known 'em a long time, Curly," he said. "Their farm was next to ours back in Kentucky. We all grew up together."

"Their family fightin' for the Union?"

"Yep, that's right. Their brother Royal's serving with McClellan. I guess he was somewhere in this last fight we had. Hope he didn't get hurt."

Tom looked up from his writing again. "I hope so too. Royal Carter is the best friend I ever had."

Then the call came down the line from Captain Majors, "All right, get the men moving, Sergeant."

Jeff grabbed his drum and moved into position, and soon the company was on its way down the road.

The action started before Jeff was ready for it. A scout came back with the information that the enemy was drawn up behind a line of trees just beyond a creek. "You can get 'em if you charge," he said. "They're not ready, I don't think, but you'll have to be quick."

Nelson Majors thought quickly. He had been watching the Union soldiers that he could see vaguely through the trees. They did seem to be unprepared. He made up his mind at once. "Private Majors, you and Private Bowers sound the charge!

104

You sergeants, see that your men hold their fire until they're in proper range! Spread out in a skirmish line!"

Jeff's blood began to rush through his veins, and his heart pounded as it always did. He began drumming the charge as loudly as he could. Charlie Bowers moved off to the other end of the line, and soon the men let out a wild yell and started across the field.

Jeff stumbled along with them, trying to stay close to his father. In case there was a command, he wanted to be able to drum it out.

As they ran, a man dropped just in front of him. It was Asa Hotchkiss, a farmer from Alabama. Jeff felt a moment's grief, for he knew that Asa was planning to go home and get married when his enlistment ran out. He was relieved to see that the man didn't seem to be hurt badly.

Then the musket balls began to whistle, and out of the trees issued a cloud of black smoke as the Federals began firing.

"Forward! Don't let 'em get away!" Captain Majors cried out. He himself was right in the front. Jeff wished he would fall back a little, but his father had told him, "Officers have to lead from the front. You can't lead from the rear!"

Now, as Jeff stumbled over the broken ground and reached the creek, he saw the bluecoats backing up. He splashed across the stream, and just as he reached the other side, a Union soldier rose up and fired. Jeff felt his hat leave his head and knew that he had escaped death by inches. At the same time, the soldier uttered a cry, grabbed his stomach, and fell.

These were the times Jeff hated. He ran on with the line of Confederate troops, and soon the enemy was routed.

Jeff leaned against a tree, breathing hard, and Tom came by. "Are you all right?"

"Just out of breath! How 'bout you?"

"Didn't get a scratch, and Pa's all right too. We lost some men, though."

To Jeff this was the saddest part of a battle. He began to wander over the battlefield, helping his comrades who had fallen. Some were wounded in a minor way and headed immediately back toward Richmond. Others had to be carried. Then Jeff came to the Union soldier who had missed his shot at him and saw that he was curled up and moaning softly.

Carefully he put down his drum and approached. He wasn't sure but that the soldier might have a pistol, but when he got there, he saw that the man's hands were red and he wasn't thinking about a weapon.

"Sorry you got hit," Jeff said, leaning over. "We'll get you to a doctor."

The soldier looked up, and his eyes were wide with fright. "I'm going to die." He gasped rather than spoke, and pain and fear twisted his face.

"Don't talk like that," Jeff said. "You'll make it."

"Are you the one that shot me?"

"No, I'm a drummer boy. I don't even carry a gun. Let me see how bad hurt you are." He pulled the soldier's hands away, and his heart sank. He'd been in enough battles to know what the chances were. The doctor said that if a soldier's got a bullet in his belly, he's a dead man.

Nevertheless Jeff began to hustle. He found Tom and explained. "Help me carry this fellow back. We've got to get him to a doctor. He's hurt bad."

Tom came and glanced down at the man and then at Jeff. Both knew that the boy had little chance. "All right," Tom said. "The doctor's got a tent set up over there. Come on, Billy Yank, we'll get you fixed up!"

The two brothers carried the moaning boy to the field hospital. When they got there and put him down, he took Jeff's arm. "Don't leave me to die," he said. "Stay with me."

Jeff hesitated, but Tom said quickly, "That's right. You stay with him, Jeff."

Jeff sat beside the soldier, and the Yankee asked his name.

When Jeff told him, he said, "My name's Josh Dawlings."

"Where you from, Josh?"

"From Maine. I wish I was back there now. I wish I'd never left." He moaned.

For more than an hour Jeff sat beside the boy until two doctors came by. They took one look at the wound, and he saw them shake their heads. "Put a dressing on it and give him something for the pain," one said.

Dawlings's eyes filled with tears, for he knew the doctors had no hope. When he was carried outside and placed beneath a tree where other wounded prisoners were being guarded, he begged Jeff, "You're the only one I know here. Stay with me, please?"

So Jeff stayed beside him, getting him water, making him as comfortable as he could.

When night came, he saw his father and asked if he could stay overnight with the boy.

"Sure, son. You do all you can. The fighting's over. The Yankees have gone back." The captain patted Josh's shoulder. "We'll take the best care of you we can, soldier. I'll leave my son here with you."

It was a terrible night for Jeff. Josh Dawlings knew his time was short. He dreaded to face death and said once, "I'm only seventeen years old. I haven't even started to live yet. I would have gotten married, maybe had children. Now none of it will ever happen."

Sometime just before dawn, Jeff dozed off. Then he heard Dawlings calling him and awakened at once. "Are you all right, Josh?" he asked.

But there was no answer except a terrible raspy sound from the wounded soldier's throat, and then he suddenly grew very still.

Jeff leaned close, and he saw that the soldier was dead. He put the boy's hands on his breast, slowly stood up, and walked away.

Back in the camp, he sat down and stared at the ground.

His father came over and sat down. "How is he?"

"He's dead."

"Too bad! Too bad! A likely looking boy."

Jeff looked up, his eyes tortured. "He should have lived, Pa. He should have had a good life."

"I know, son, I know. I think that about every man that we lose and the men they lose too. I think about your mother. I think about Esther. I think about all our family, scattered now." He seemed very sad.

Jeff sat thinking for a long time. Finally he said, "Pa, I've had hard feelings against Leah. We had a fight."

"I'm sorry to hear that," the captain said. "Friends don't need to be fighting. There's enough misery in this world without losing our friends. You know one of my favorite Scriptures?"

"What's that?"

"'A friend loveth at all times.' That's good, isn't it? That means when I don't behave right, my friends still love me. When I do 'em wrong, they love me anyhow. 'A friend loveth at all times.' That's the best description of love I know."

Jeff nodded slowly. "I'll make it up to Leah, Pa. I promise I will. I'm sorry."

"We all go wrong sometimes, son. The thing is, when you see what you've done, do your best to make it right."

12

God Meant It for Good

Rufus Prather stepped up onto the front porch and knocked on the door. When Leah came to ask, "Yes, what is it?" he said, "Sure am thirsty. Maybe you could give me a glass of tea?"

Leah hesitated, but the boy was useful at times. "All right, Rufus, come on in." As she led him to the kitchen she said, "We don't have any real tea—just sassafras."

"That'll go down mighty good." Rufus grinned.

When they reached the kitchen he sat down and watched while she poured a glassful. He drank it down thirstily. "That was mighty good," he said. "How 'bout another one?" As he started on the second glass, Uncle Silas came in.

"Why, hello, Mr. Carter," Rufus said. "How you feeling these days?"

"Very well, Rufus. How about you?"

"Oh, finer'n frog hair." He waved his hand around. He was a lazy boy, but he loved to talk. "If words was work," someone had said of him, "he'd be the workingest young fellow in the country!"

Leah began to make a piecrust, as Rufus talked on. He traveled around a great deal, always glad to run errands to get out of work on the farm. He knew everybody and was a great gossip. This time, however, he did have some news.

"Did you hear what happened last night?"

"No, what was it?" Silas asked, pouring himself some tea.

"Why, some of them Yankee officers in Libby Prison escaped."

"Escaped!" Leah said. "How'd they do that?"

"Dunno, but they did. Six of 'em." He drank his sassafras tea noisily, then eyed the piecrust. "What sort of pie you making? Apple, I hope. That's my favorite."

"No, all we've got is dried peaches. Tell us more about the escape."

"All I heard was that the Secretary of War is threatenin' to shoot the warden there at Libby Prison. Wouldn't be surprised but what he might do it too. He sure does hate for any prisoners to get away."

He looked up and inquired, "Haven't you heard patrols going up and down the road this morning?"

Silas Carter nodded slowly. "There was a patrol went by early today, but they didn't stop here."

"Well, they're chasing those Yankee officers, you can bet on it. And if they catch 'em, they'll handle 'em pretty rough, you bet."

Uncle Silas asked cautiously, "Are they coming back this way?"

"I reckon they are. When I was over at Crawfordville, they was going into houses, and people was pretty mad too." He grinned at Leah and winked. "You ain't hiding no Yankee officers in the attic, are you, Leah?"

"No," Leah said abruptly. Her hands were trembling on the piecrust.

"Well, something else happened. You know Lincoln—he called them three hundred thousand men to serve for three years?"

111

"Yes, I heard about that," Silas said. "What about it?"

"Well, he didn't get 'em." Rufus laughed gleefully. "He cut the time back to nine months, and even then he didn't get 'em. I don't guess you could spare one of them peaches, could you, Miss Leah?"

Silently Leah gave him a dried peach, and he chewed noisily. "I'll tell you what Lincoln *didn't* do. He had a chance to get two regiments of black soldiers—I forget what state—and he turned 'em down cold. That shows how much Yankees think of Negroes. Won't even use 'em for soldiers. Lincoln's got more sense than that, I reckon."

For what seemed an hour, Rufus Prather sat talking. At last he got up reluctantly and said, "Well, I guess I'd better get back, or Mr. Driscoll'll have my hide. Thanks for the tea."

He left the house, and as soon as Leah heard the wagon move out, she said, "That's bad, isn't it, Uncle Silas?"

"I think it might be. It's dangerous enough the way it's been, but with patrols moving around, I just don't see any hope. How is Ezra?"

"Oh, he's better. I'm going to go out and see how he is today—and take him something to eat."

She left the house with a plate of pork chops, boiled cabbage, and cornpone and the pitcher of sassafras tea.

When she stepped inside the barn, as usual Ezra was there to meet her. "Dinnertime already?" he asked.

"Yes, sit down and eat. I'll have maybe a peach pie tonight."

Ezra's appetite had returned, and he ate all that she had brought him and drank a great deal of the sassafras tea. "We never had anything like this tea you make. Sure is good," he commented.

"I'm glad you like it, Ezra." She gave him a curious look and saw that his eyes were bright. There was no more fever. He moved much easier and seemed alert. "You're better, aren't you?"

"Yes, sure am. Seems like yesterday I just got better all at once." He took a deep breath and stretched his chest out. "Sure feels good to feel good again."

For a while they talked, but apparently he could see she was disturbed. He asked, "What's the matter, Leah? Something's wrong."

Leah bit her lip, wondering whether she should tell him about the escape. She decided it would only be fair. "Some Federal officers escaped from Libby Prison, Ezra. The government's mad about it. They've got orders out to find them, no matter what. Rufus Prather came by and told us about it."

Ezra turned the glass around in his hands. He took the last swallow of tea and nodded. "I've been watching through cracks in the barn. I saw a patrol go by. Cavalry, some of it. They was moving slow, not like soldiers usually move. I wondered what they were doing. Now I guess I know."

Leah moved her hands nervously over her hair. She said quietly, "It makes things harder for us."

Ezra gave her a sharp glance. "Yes, it does. Time for me to get out of here."

"No! Now would be the worst time. Those patrols will be everywhere, and people are looking for prisoners. It would have been better if you had gone before, but you weren't able."

"Well, I can't stay here. I've got to try it."

He got up slowly, and Leah stood in front of him. He smiled, and she noticed again what a nice smile he had. He was very little taller than she was and seemed not at all like the fierce Yankee soldiers that the South had portrayed.

Suddenly Ezra reached for her hand.

Surprised, she put it in his.

He held it for a moment and said, "You've been mighty good to me, Leah." He raised her hand and kissed it and then laughed shortly. "I never did that before."

Leah took her hand back, her cheeks red. "Neither did I."

They stood silently, embarrassed by the moment, and then Ezra said, "I thought it was pretty hard going to prison, losing out on everything. And when I was so sick and thought I was going to die, I thought God didn't care." He added quietly, "But I guess God knows all about us. I reckon He brought me to this place so I could find out about Jesus. Now that I have, it won't be so hard going back."

"Oh, Ezra, I wish you didn't have to go."

"Well, I've got to get away from here. That's all there is to it. I can't get you and your uncle in trouble. Not after all you've done for me." He frowned. "I don't think it's likely we'll see each other again, so this is good-bye."

Leah said, "Don't do anything just yet. Let me talk to Uncle Silas first. Do you promise?"

Ezra looked at her curiously and cocked his head to one side. "Sure, I promise. I'm not going anywhere until after dark, but I don't see how he can do anything."

"You remember the Bible story I read you about Joseph?"

114

"I sure do. That was a good one."

"You remember where he wound up after his brothers sold him?"

"Why, sure. He was in jail, and he didn't do anything wrong."

"That's right. But later on, in the last of that story, he told his brothers, 'When you sold me, you meant it for bad, but God meant it for good. He sent me before you to prepare the way.'

"Don't you see, sometimes bad things seem so awful, and we just want to cry and kick and scream, but if we could just believe that God lets these things come—for His own good reasons—I think we'd be better off."

She turned and left the barn.

The young man went back and sat down on the hay. "She sure is some gal," he murmured to himself.

13
Silas Gets a Plan

Leah and Uncle Silas stayed up late, talking about the problem, trying to find a way out. But no matter what they thought of, the situation seemed hopeless.

Then Silas said, "Let's pray about it, Leah. It looks like it's going to take God to get us out of this one." He asked softly, "You've gotten pretty fond of that young Yankee, haven't you?"

Leah flushed. "Oh, don't be silly, Uncle Silas. He just was so helpless." She half laughed at herself, adding, "I used to take in every sick kitten that came around the farm. Everybody laughed at me for it."

"I don't reckon that young fellow's gonna be laughing. You sure saved his bacon. Well, maybe we'll think of something tonight. I don't plan on sleeping much."

Leah lay awake for what seemed hours. Her thoughts swarmed, and all she could think of was something bad happening. She thought of Ezra trying to escape and being shot. She thought about the patrols finding him in the barn. And she thought about what would befall Uncle Silas and her if that happened. At last she just said wearily, "Lord, I can't even think anymore, but I ask You to help Ezra. Help Uncle Silas and me to get him out of this somehow." Then she drifted off to sleep.

She was awakened some time later by Silas calling for her. "Leah! Leah!"

Opening her eyes in alarm, she saw that dawn was beginning to lighten the eastern skies. She jumped out of bed, grabbed her robe, and put it on as she ran.

She found her uncle standing in the middle of the living room. His hair was rumpled, and he was running his fingers through his beard as he did when he was excited.

"What is it, Uncle Silas? What's wrong?"

"Wrong?" Silas grinned at her. "Why, nothing's wrong. Everything's right."

Leah stared at him. "You mean you found a way to get Ezra out of here?"

"I guess I didn't sleep two hours last night." Silas shook his head, and his voice filled with wonder. "Must have made up a hundred and five different plans, all of them bad. Then finally, I just gave up, and I said, 'Lord, You'll have to do it.'"

"Why, that's what I did," Leah said, wonder in her voice too. "But I still didn't think of anything."

"Well, it was a funny thing. As soon as I woke up this morning—you know how it is when you're not quite awake, not quite asleep, sort of both? Well, there I was, and all of a sudden this plan popped in my mind, just as clear as if I was seeing it on a printed page."

"About Ezra?"

"Yes, about Ezra—and about you too, Leah. Sit down. Let me tell you about it." Then he said, "No, go get Ezra and bring him into the house."

"But isn't that dangerous? Somebody might see him."

"It's part of my plan. Go get him."

Leah ran back to her room and changed into her clothes. She hurried so fast that she almost stumbled over a shoelace she left untied. "I'll be right back," she called to her uncle.

She left the house at a run, stepped inside the barn, and called, "Ezra! Ezra! Come here, quick!"

"What is it?" Ezra almost slid down the stairs. He was fully dressed, even wearing his shoes. "What's wrong?"

"Nothing's wrong, but Uncle Silas says he's got a plan. Come on!"

She took his hand, and they ran across the yard. It was just growing light. She glanced apprehensively at the road, but no one was stirring. "Come on in the house, quick!"

As soon as they were in the living room, Ezra looked around and said, "First time I've ever been in this part of the house. All I ever did was steal food out of the kitchen."

Silas said, "You must be a quiet-footed fellow and nervy too, coming into a house where you knew there were folks."

"I guess if a fellow gets hungry enough, he'll try anything."

"Here now! You two sit down. I want to talk to you. I think maybe I've got something that'll work." He waited until they were seated, then he sat down in front of them. "You ever hear of a fellow called Edgar Allen Poe?"

Ezra shook his head. "Nope, never heard of him."

Leah said, "I think I have, but I can't remember where."

"He writes stories—sometimes they're in the paper."

"Oh! I remember them now. Some of them are just awful."

"They sure are," Uncle Silas agreed. "But he wrote one that I thought was the best thing I ever read. The name of it was—I forget the name of it. Something about a letter." His eyes were bright with excitement, and he looked over at Ezra. "Now our problem is, we've got to hide you. Isn't that right?"

"Yes, sir. That's right."

"Well, what do people do when they hide things?"

Leah thought quickly. "They put them in a place where nobody will look for them."

Silas pounded the arms of his chair, "Right, but that's exactly the places people *do* look. I mean, if they came in looking for a place where we might hide money, they'd look in the drawers or the chest. They'd look for a box under the bed. They'd look under the mattress, because that's where people put money they're trying to hide." He grinned at them and said, "But what if you put it in a place where they'd never think to look?"

"I don't understand," Leah said, puzzled.

"Well, in this story a man had to hide a letter. He couldn't get rid of it, had to keep it. He knew the police would be coming to search for it. And they did come, but they didn't find the letter."

"Where'd he hide it, Mr. Carter?" Ezra asked.

"You won't believe this, but he left it right out on the table with some other letters. He kept his letters in this little holder out in the open, and he just stuck it right in the middle of 'em."

"Why, I don't understand," Leah repeated. "Didn't they look at the letters?"

119

"No, they didn't, and that was the point of the story. Nobody dreamed he'd be dumb enough to leave a valuable letter out like that, so they tore the house apart, and they didn't find a thing."

Leah was a quick-witted girl. She looked over at her uncle and then glanced at Ezra. She said slowly, "So you're saying we should really stop trying to *hide* Ezra."

"That's exactly right, and that's exactly what we're going to do—if you've got the nerve for it, young man."

Ezra smiled. "Well, if it's any chance at all, it's more than I've got now. I could never escape by myself, I know that. Right here next to Richmond with about a million Confederate soldiers everywhere you look. Exactly how do you plan to do this?"

"All right. Here's what we'll do. Tomorrow you two are going to get dressed up. You're gonna take a load of grain in to town and sell it to the commissary."

"Sell it to the army?" Leah asked in astonishment.

"That's right, and you're going to get a receipt from them, and you're going to tell them you're from Kentucky and you want to go back there and get some more grain."

Leah let this run through her mind. Finally she asked, "But what if somebody asks who Ezra is?"

"Who's gonna ask? Do you go up to young fellers and ask them who they are?"

"Well, no," Leah admitted, "but I'm not a soldier on patrol. Why, they'll take one look at him—"

"They would if he was wearing that Federal uniform, but he won't be wearing *that*. He'll be wearing just regular clothes—my clothes. We're about the same size, so he'll put them on, and you two will go. They're pretty hungry, the army's horses are. There hasn't been enough feed. They'll be glad to get a wagonload, and they'll be even more glad if you tell them more's coming."

"Let me get this straight," Leah said. "We sell them the grain, we get a receipt. Then if anybody stops us, we show them that receipt."

"That's right. You can even ask them for a pass to get you through the lines until you're through to where the Union troops are." He smiled. "You won't even have to lie. You do live in Kentucky, Leah, and you can bring some grain back. Of course—" he looked at Ezra then "—you won't be coming back with this young fellow. But they won't notice that."

Now Ezra shook his head. "It's risky, Mr. Carter. Why, if they caught me, Leah'd be caught too. I just can't—"

"Now, son," Silas Carter said, "I believe the Lord's made me think of this. I sure couldn't think of anything else, and neither could Leah. And I believe it'll work. I just want you to promise me one thing. Don't go back in the army. That's what they do all the time—a soldier 'gives his parole,' that is, he promises not to fight if they release him."

"I'll be glad to promise that," Ezra said. "I've had enough of this war to do me."

"All right, that's what we'll do then. We'll have to buy the grain, but I know Cy Dinwittie has got some he wants to sell. You take the wagon over tomorrow, Leah. Get it, come back here, pick up Ezra, and the two of you will be off."

* * *

121

The next day went exactly as Silas had out-lined it. Leah got up, dressed, and packed her extra clothes. She went over to Mr. Dinwittie's, bought the grain, and returned. When she got back to Rich-mond Manor, she pulled up in front of the house.

A young man came out, and she almost fell off the wagon with surprise. She'd only seen Ezra wearing old ragged clothes. Now he wore a good, sound pair of brown trousers, a clean white shirt with a string tie, a black hat with a wide brim, and a pair of almost-new brown boots. He did look a little pale from his long imprisonment.

"Ezra! I never would have known you."

Ezra laughed sheepishly, "Never had such nice clothes in all my life." He turned around, as Uncle Silas came onto the porch, and said, "Mr. Carter, sure do thank you for all you've done for me."

Silas put his hand out and shook the boy's. "God go with you, my boy. You always follow the Lord, you hear me?" Then he turned to Leah and took her in his arms. He kissed her cheek and whis-pered, "And you come back, you hear me?"

"Are you really well enough? Will you be all right until I get back?"

"Yes, I'll be fine. Don't take any chances."

And the two got in the wagon and made their way to Richmond, Ezra driving the team.

As they approached the commissary, Leah said, "Are you scared?"

"Not a bit!"

"Well, I am!"

"Don't worry, Leah. It's going to be all right. You wait and see if it isn't."

He drew up in front of the commissary, and a corporal came over to ask, "You bring that grain to sell it?"

"Yes, sir, sure did."

The corporal nodded. "We need all we can get. Pull right over there. The quartermaster will be out to weigh it and pay you."

Ten minutes later a lieutenant walked out and looked at the wagonload of grain. He named the price they were giving, and Ezra said at once, "That's fine, Lieutenant."

The officer said, "Come on in the office then. I'll pay you while they unload the wagon."

The lieutenant sat down at his desk, opened a drawer, and paid them cash from a box of Confederate money.

Leah said, "Could you use some more grain, Lieutenant?"

"Could we! All you've got!"

"Well, I live over in Kentucky. We've got to go back there. We'll be glad to bring you another load."

"Kentucky? That's a long way."

"Yes, it is, but that's where home is. And relatives and all."

"Well, you'll need a pass. Let me make it out for you."

Leah turned and met the eyes of the young Union soldier.

He was smiling.

When they got outside, Ezra said, "You see, I told you it'd be all right."

Leah laughed nervously. "You've got more faith than I have already, Ezra."

He helped her into the wagon. "I guess we'd better get started." He spoke to the horses, and they moved out smartly.

The guard on the outside of town stopped them, and they showed him their receipt and their permit. He took one careless look at the signature and said, "Pass," and they left the city of Richmond, headed for Kentucky.

One thing they did not notice, and that was Rufus. The fat boy had been loafing downtown, and when Leah and Ezra rode out of the city, he spotted them.

Well, now, who is that feller—and where are they gettin' off to? he wondered.

14

Lucy Smells a Rat

The first thing Silas noticed when he went back into the house was a letter lying on the kitchen table. "I never saw that before. I reckon Leah must have left it for me."

He picked up the envelope and saw that with it was a note. He pulled his glasses out, put them on, and read.

> Uncle Silas, I feel like I must get word to Jeff about what's happening. Would you please see that he gets this letter? I've written it so that no one who reads it will understand what I'm doing except Jeff.

That was all the note said, and Silas held it in his hand for a moment. "Don't see how I can get this letter to the boy. I'm not able to go to town."

He waited all morning for somebody he knew to go by on the road, but no one did. But then he looked out and saw Rufus Prather ambling back toward the Driscoll home. Going to the door, he called, "Rufus, come here!"

Rufus looked up and sauntered over. When he got to the porch, he said, "Yes, sir? What'll it be?"

"Rufus, I've got a very important errand. I'll pay you five dollars if you'll go to the camp and see this gets to the right person."

Rufus took the letter and stared at it. "Well, I can't read. Who does it go to?"

"Take it to the Stonewall Brigade. Give it an officer there named Capt. Nelson Majors. It's for his son Jeff, but he'll see he gets it."

"Oh, the soldier boy that went to the party with Leah."

"That's right. Will you do it?"

"I guess so."

The matter was urgent, so Silas hesitated but then said, "There'll be another five dollars if you can get it done right away. Stop by on your way back, and I'll give it to you."

"Why, I'll do that! I can use ten dollars."

Rufus left Silas Carter's house and headed back toward Richmond. He caught a ride in a wagon, but it was not going out to the camp. When he dismounted, he said, "Thanks for the lift," and then started walking.

He'd not gone far when he saw Lucy Driscoll coming out of a shop. He knew she had little use for him, but he stopped to say, "Howdy, Miss Lucy."

"Oh, hello, Rufus. What are you doing in town? I thought you were supposed to be on your way home."

"Well, I was, but Mr. Carter asked me to deliver this letter out to camp."

Lucy's eyes sharpened, and Rufus noticed. He had heard about the party from one of the servants. "You didn't take to the Carter girl, did you? So I heard."

"You hear too much, Rufus. It's just that she's not a true Southerner."

"Well, she's a mighty pretty Yankee girl, if that's what she is. She knows how to catch the good-looking fellers too. Why, I saw her earlier today down at the commissary. She was with a fine-looking young feller. I don't know who he was, though." He winked at her and said, "You might take lessons on how to catch a man from that gal."

Lucy scowled, and a quick answer leaped to her lips. But then a thought came to her. *What young man would Leah be riding in a wagon with?* She was instantly suspicious. *After all, she's not a true Southern girl. I'd like to know who that man was she was with. If Rufus doesn't know him, he couldn't be from around here. Rufus knows everybody.*

Brightly she said, "You got to walk all the way out to the camp?"

"Yep, it's for a soldier there—that young soldier boy you were so sweet on—Jeff. I'm supposed to give it to his daddy."

Lucy said, "Oh, no point in you walking all that way. I'll be going out to camp anyway in the buggy. Give it to me."

Rufus looked at her suspiciously. She'd never done anything nice for him before, but it was a long three-mile walk to the camp, and he was tired. "All right. Be sure you do it."

"Oh, I will."

As soon as Rufus turned and headed back out of town, Lucy went to one side and looked at the letter. It was sealed with wax, but she thought, *It wouldn't be wrong to open it if she's doing something she shouldn't.* She opened the letter and read it.

Dear Jeff,

I know you've been worried about me and you think what I'm doing isn't right. I have to do it. I'll be leaving Richmond for a while and then I hope our problem will be all solved. I want us to be friends again, like we used to be. Don't worry about me. Stop by and see my uncle if you can. I'm going to Kentucky, but I'll be back soon.

It was signed, "Leah," and there was a P.S.

We'll be stopping tonight at the Seven Point Creek. That's where you and I stopped when we first came here. You won't be with me tonight, but I'll be thinking of you at the Creek.

Lucy thought hard. *She's leaving town with somebody, and she doesn't want anybody to know who it is, or she'd have said so.*

She'd heard the rumors about the Carter girls, Sarah and Leah, being accused of spying. Sarah had actually been tried for it, and the man that had accused her had been to the Driscoll home several times. She thought for a minute and said, "Captain Lyons! That was his name. I'm going to him with this letter."

Capt. Wesley Lyons looked surprised when a young lady walked into his office. He stood up at once, recognizing her. "Why, it's Miss Driscoll, isn't it?"

"That's right, Captain Lyons. You were at our house two weeks ago at the ball."

"Yes, I was. Delightful time I had too. Won't you sit down?"

"No, I really don't have time, Captain Lyons. I'm wondering if I should be here at all. You see, I have a problem."

"Well, anything I can do to help, just let me know."

"It's like this. I remember hearing about the trouble you had with those two girls that were staying with Mr. Carter."

She saw at once that Lyons was still angry over the affair. She knew he had been rebuked by his superiors for bringing charges. True, he had succeeded in getting Sarah evicted from the South, but he had expected to see her imprisoned. He still thought she was guilty. "What about those girls?" he demanded, almost harshly.

"Well, the youngest one, Leah Carter—I know her slightly. She has a friend in the Stonewall Brigade. His name is Jeff Majors."

"Yes, I know Captain Majors. What about this girl?"

"There's something wrong about her, I think. She's not true to the Confederacy."

"I don't doubt it for a minute," the captain snapped. "She should have been sent out of Richmond along with her sister." He peered at her curiously, "Why have you come to me?"

"It's this letter. Mr. Carter gave it to a boy that works for us. It's from Leah Carter, and it's to Captain Majors's son. I opened it. And I suppose you think that's wrong."

"Opened it? Why would you do that?"

Lucy said stubbornly, "I think she's a spy, just like her sister was."

This caught the captain's attention. "May I see the letter?"

"Yes, but you won't be able to make much out of it. I know this—she's leaving town with a stranger, and there have been some men who have escaped —some officers, haven't there? I think it's one of them she's trying to get away with."

Lyons scanned the letter. "This doesn't say anything that could convict her. I'd have to catch her with the man."

"Well, I didn't know what to do, so I came to you."

"You did the right thing, young lady. You leave this to me. This creek—Seven Point—they'll be there tonight. I'll have a patrol out there to intercept them. If she does have a Yankee officer with her, you can rest assured he'll be captured, and this time Miss Carter won't get away!"

15

A Wild Ride

The Stonewall Brigade wound its way back into Richmond, exhausted and hungry. Jeff was still sad because of the death of the young Union soldier. He said little to anyone but went about his duties quietly.

His father approached him early the next morning. "Here's a letter for you, Jeff."

Jeff tore open the envelope and stared at the letter. "It's from Leah," he said finally.

His father, probably seeing that he was disturbed, asked gently, "Anything I can do to help?"

Jeff shook his head slowly. He knew exactly what Leah had planned and wished there were a way he could help. "No, sir, I don't suppose so."

"Well, I think you deserve a break. Why don't you go into town and see if you can find a razor for me? I've looked everywhere, but that's another thing the blockade's cut off. I'm gonna have to raise a crop of whiskers if I don't find one."

"Yes, sir, I'll do my best."

Jeff made his way into town where he went from shop to shop for more than an hour.

Finally he found a used razor, but the price was twenty dollars Confederate money. He raised his eyebrows. "That's mighty expensive. That's too much to pay for a razor."

The shopkeeper shrugged his shoulders. "If you got two dollars Union money, I'll take that."

This was the usual exchange at the time. The Confederacy might be at war with the North, but shopkeepers, bankers, and those who dealt in trade knew well the worthlessness of Confederate currency. It had been printed up hurriedly without any backing, with merely a promise to pay, and already the government was strained in every direction from carrying on the war.

"It'll have to do." Jeff handed the cash over and walked out of the shop. He was headed back toward camp when he saw Lucy in a carriage driven by one of the Driscoll slaves.

"Jeff! Jeff! Wait a minute!"

He halted and went over to where the carriage had drawn up beside the street. "Hello, Lucy. How are you?"

"Jeff! I've got to talk to you." She turned to the driver and said, "Matthew, leave us alone." She waited until the driver crawled down out of the buggy and wandered slowly off toward the shops.

"Get up in the buggy, Jeff," Lucy said. "I've got something to tell you, and I don't think you're going to like it much."

Staring at her, Jeff asked, "What is it?" He had no idea in the world what the girl had in her mind. She looked pretty, as usual, wearing a dark green dress with a bonnet to match, but he was not in the mood to appreciate beauty. The battle had grieved him, as battles always did.

"Jeff! I know you are friends with Leah Carter, but there's something going on. There's something *funny* going on."

At once Jeff grew wary. *Uh-oh*, he thought, *I hope she hasn't found out about that Union prisoner.* "What is it, Lucy?" he asked quickly.

"Well, earlier today I found Rufus in town. He had a letter he was supposed to deliver to your father."

"Yes, I got it. What about it?"

"Well, I offered to carry the letter, and when Rufus gave it to me to take out to camp, he told me he saw Leah and a strange man in a wagon headed out of Richmond. Rufus knows everybody in this county. All he does is gossip and watch people. He said he never saw the man before, and I think he was one of those Yankee prisoners that escaped from Libby."

"Oh, that's not right," Jeff protested. "Those prisoners would be hiding out in the woods. They wouldn't get right out in the open."

"Maybe they would, if they had somebody to help them escape. And then that letter! I don't understand all of it, but something's going on." She gave Jeff a curious glance and said, "What about those girls? She and her sister were suspected of being spies. Captain Lyons told me so."

"Wesley Lyons?"

"Yes!" Lucy grew excited. "I just *know* she's a spy, Jeff, so I read the letter and took it to Captain Lyons, and he said he was going to do something about it."

"You shouldn't have done that, Lucy!" Jeff exclaimed.

The girl stared at him. "Why not? If she's a spy, she needs to be caught and put in prison. Isn't that right?"

Jeff wanted to protest, but he suddenly knew he had to play a part. "Why . . . sure, I guess that's right. I just wasn't thinking, Lucy." He sat there talking, but his mind was racing ahead. As soon as he could, he touched his cap and said, "Well, I've got to get back to camp. Orders you know."

"Come and see me as soon as you can," Lucy said. "We can work on this, Jeff. Together. Wouldn't it be exciting if we caught a spy!"

"It sure would. Well, I'll see you later, Lucy."

Jeff made himself amble away, but as soon as he was out of sight of the girl, he ran halfway back to camp.

He found his father and gasped, "Pa, Leah's in some kind of trouble. I've got to go help her!"

"Can you tell me about it, son?"

Jeff hesitated, then nodded. "Yes, sir, I think you better know." Quickly he sketched what had gone on, and he saw his father's brow furrow. He ended by saying, "What I think is, Leah's taking that soldier back through the lines in that wagon. Somehow she thinks she can get him away."

"Well, what can you do, son?"

"Her letter said they're going to be at Seven Point Creek tonight. I bet Wesley Lyons will send a troop there. If I can get there before they do, I can warn them."

Captain Majors thought hard for a moment. "All right. I think this is serious. I'll draw a horse for you from the cavalry supply, a good one. You'll have to be careful, though. Horses are precious these days. Come on."

An hour later Jeff swung into the saddle and pulled his hat down. "I'll get the horse back safe, Captain. Don't worry." He spurred the animal, a fine chestnut stallion, and rode off at a gallop.

I'm getting a late start, he thought as he cantered out of town toward the outer lines. He had a pass signed by his father, so he had no trouble getting by the sentries. In any case, they would not have stopped a Confederate soldier. He rode hard again and tried to think what he would do if he saw the patrol. "I can't let 'em see me. I've got to get around 'em somehow."

He rode hard until two o'clock, when he stopped at a farmhouse to get a drink of water and to rest his horse.

"Have you seen any troops moving along the road, ma'am?" He drank gratefully from the gourd dipper, savoring the cold water out of the well. "A Confederate unit?"

"Well, yeah, you just missed them, Private." The woman had a pair of bright blue eyes, and she smiled as she pointed down the road. "They stopped here about thirty minutes ago. I heard one of them say they was headed for the river."

"That'd be Seven Point, wouldn't it?"

"That's right. It ain't far. I expect you can catch 'em time they get there. There's a shortcut, if you want to take it." She quickly described a little-used road that cut around the main highway. "You'll come out right on Seven Point. You might even be waiting for them soldier friends of yours."

"Thanks a lot."

He got into the saddle and spurred the big chestnut. A quarter of a mile down the road he saw the large oak where the narrow road angled off. He found it to be little more than a trail, barely wide enough for a wagon. The going was rough, but he did not slow his horse.

From time to time, he ducked a branch and once was almost raked out of the saddle by one. It hit him in the face and gashed his right cheek. As he drove the horse on, he felt the blood trickling

135

down and fumbled for a handkerchief. He wiped the wound as best he could and then paid it no more heed.

The road made several turns, but finally he reached a stream where there was no bridge. "This must be Seven Point," he said. The trail turned to the left, and he took it, thinking, *This has got to lead to the bridge on the main road.*

His horse was tired and reluctant, but Jeff lifted him into a gallop, saying, "We've *got* to get there before those soldiers!"

16
Jeff Saves the Day

This sure is nice, ain't it, Leah?"

Leah looked over toward Ezra from where she was frying bacon in a pan. They had camped beside the bridge, knowing it would soon be dark. "Yes, it is," she said, glancing around. "I thought we'd make better time, but I guess we'll be out of danger tomorrow."

"That bacon sure smells good. Can I help you with the cooking?"

"No, you made the fire. I'll do the cooking." She quickly threw a meal together. She had changed clothes and was wearing a brown dress now, and she'd loosed her hair so that it fell down her back. He'd never seen hair like hers. *Almost like spun gold*, he thought.

She expertly fried the bacon, then broke the four eggs that she had brought packed in a jar of sand. "You like yours scrambled or fried?"

"I like 'em any way I can get 'em." Ezra grinned. He picked up the tin plates, and, when she had fried the eggs carefully, she slipped them onto the plates.

They sat down then, and she handed him some biscuits.

Ezra said, "I seen Christian people ask the blessing. Reckon we could do that here?"

Leah smiled at him. "Of course, we can. Do you want to do it, Ezra?"

137

The young man looked startled. "Well, I ain't had much practice, but I guess I got to start some-time, don't I?" He bowed his head, as did Leah, and was silent for a moment.

Then he said, "Lord, thank You for these eggs. They sure look good. And You know how I like ba-con. I appreciate that too. And especially for these good biscuits Leah has made, Lord. There ain't no-body can make biscuits better than her as You probably know. Anyway, I'm grateful for all these vittles, and I thank You best I know how. Amen."

Leah echoed, "Amen." There was a smile on her lips. "That was good, Ezra. I'm proud of you."

"Well, I'm getting a late start. I aim to do the best I can."

They ate quickly, and Leah poured some cof-fee. "This'll be the last of this we'll have," she said. "I borrowed just a little from what we had. Uncle Silas, he sure loves coffee. I tried to make some out of acorns, but it tasted awful."

Ezra sipped his coffee cautiously and nodded. "This is good." Then he leaned back and looked up at the sky, which was growing darker. "Pretty to-night, ain't it?" He looked over at her. "I guess you'll be glad to see your folks back in Kentucky?"

"Oh, yes, I miss them so much, and I'm anx-ious to see Esther too."

"Esther? Now who is she?"

"That's Jeff's baby sister. His mother died giv-ing birth to her, so we're keeping her until the war's over."

Ezra found that interesting. He sat staring into the fire, poking it with a stick. "That's real nice, her being a Confederate baby."

Leah laughed suddenly.

Her laugh made a delightful sound, he thought.

"Oh, Ezra, she's not a Confederate. She's not anything except a baby."

"Why, I guess that's right, ain't it? Babies are just babies." He pushed his hair back from his forehead. "Be nice if we could stay that way—no Rebels, no Yankees, just people."

Leah sighed. "It'll be that way one day."

"What do you reckon you'll do when the war is over?"

"Why, there's not much for a woman to do, is there? I'll get married and have a family."

Her words caught at Ezra, and he sipped his coffee thoughtfully. "Well, whoever gets you, Leah, will get the best there is. You can already cook and take care of a house, and you're the prettiest girl I ever saw. Course, I ain't seen many girls."

She laughed again. "You sure know how to spoil a compliment. I don't know—" She halted abruptly. "Listen! Someone's coming!"

They stood up, and Ezra turned toward his left. "Rider coming from that way!" He listened. "It's only one—but he's sure coming hard!" He hesitated, then said, "I don't think it'd be anybody looking for us—not just one man."

The two stood listening as the hoofbeats got louder.

Suddenly a horse appeared from around the bend, the rider bending over him, and Ezra tensed.

"Leah!"

The horseman pulled up, and Leah looked at him. "Jeff!" she cried. "What are *you* doing here?"

"No time for that! The patrol's ten minutes behind me!" He looked over at Ezra. "Payne, you've

139

got to hide yourself. They've got evidence that Leah's leaving with a escaped Yankee prisoner."

"They *know* about me?"

"No, they don't know about you, but they know some prisoners have escaped." He looked at Leah and said, "It was Lucy. She read the note that you sent to me, and Rufus saw you two leaving."

"I've got to get out of here!" Ezra cried in alarm.

He was about to run, but Jeff said, "Look! Take my horse—ride on down the road a ways. Stay out of sight. When they leave, I'll come and get you."

"I never rode a horse before."

"Well, you're about to learn. Here, just put your foot here." Jeff hoisted the young man into the saddle and handed him the reins. "Just hang onto him. Pull to the right to go right and left to go left and back when you want to stop. Git!" He slapped the chestnut on the side, and the horse trotted away down the road.

"But what about you, Jeff? They mustn't find you here either."

Jeff seemed so relieved at beating the patrol that he was able to smile. "Sure they can. They know you've got someone with you, but they don't know who it is. I've got papers, and they're not going to arrest a Confederate soldier, I don't think." He looked down at the remains of the supper and said, "We've got to be natural. Why don't you cook me up some eggs or something quick so I can be eating when they come?"

Quickly Leah pulled some more bacon from the pack and put the skillet back on the fire. "Here, you just sit down, Jeff," she said. She glanced down the road. "Are you sure they're coming?"

"Yes, and we've got to get our story straight too. I'm going to Kentucky with you to bring this wagon back. That's the story."

"All right. That's what we'll tell 'em then."

She barely had time to prepare a meal for Jeff, and he was still eating when he looked up, saying, "I reckon that's them coming down the road now."

Leah listened. "What do we do, Jeff?"

"Nothing. Let me do most of the talking, though."

They were sitting there when a patrol of six Confederate cavalrymen pulled up.

A sergeant dismounted and handed the lines of his horse to one of his troopers. He came forward, his eyes watchful. "Hello!" he said.

"Hello, Sergeant," Jeff said, "you're riding a little late tonight, aren't you?"

The sergeant seemed a bit taken aback by Jeff's uniform. "I'm Sergeant Buchanan, from Richmond." He studied the two, then asked, "You been on the road long?"

"We sold some feed to the quartermaster early this morning. Headed back now to get another load."

Sergeant Buchanan asked, "You mind showing me the papers that they always give at the commissary?"

"Oh, I have them over here," Leah said. She went to a sack that was in the wagon and pulled out a paper. "Here it is, Sergeant, and here is the pass that the lieutenant gave us."

Sergeant Buchanan took the papers, held them up to the firelight, and peered at them closely. "They look all right," he said.

"What's the trouble, Sergeant? Something wrong?" Jeff asked lazily. He put another chunk of biscuit in his mouth and chewed it as if he hadn't a care in the world. "You're not looking for the Yankees to attack here, are you?"

"No, nothing like that, Private." Sergeant Buchanan handed back the papers and stood there uncertainly. "What's your unit, Private, and your business out here?"

"Stonewall Brigade."

The sergeant straightened up. "Stonewall Brigade? Well, I hear tell you're getting ready to go into action against Pope. He's coming down the Shenandoah."

"I think that's right. My father's captain of A Company. He says we've got to be ready to move at any time." He took another bite of biscuit and washed it down with coffee. "I just had to see this young lady home. She lives down that way a piece, and I've got to bring back another load of grain."

The sergeant seemed to relax. "Well, we need all the feed we can get. These horses are living on nothing but grass." He touched his hat, then said, "Just checking." He turned and went back to his horse. Stepping into his saddle, he said, "All right, let's head back. It'll be a long ride, but I want to be back in town tonight. Good night!"

Leah and Jeff sat there tensely, and finally Jeff let out his breath. "Well," he said, "I reckon that's that."

Leah found that her hands were trembling. "I was really scared, Jeff," she confessed. "How'd you know we'd be here?"

"Well, you said so in the letter."

"Oh, that's right. I forgot." She looked down the road. "We'd better go get Ezra. He's not very good with a horse."

They walked down the road a short distance, and when Leah called out they heard a faint answer. They stood waiting, and soon Ezra appeared —leading the horse, not riding him.

"It's all right, Ezra. They're gone."

Ezra handed the reins to Jeff. "I guess I owe you a lot, Jeff," he said. "They'd of got us sure if you hadn't come."

Jeff stared at the Yankee soldier, then shrugged. "Come on back. We'll talk about what we've got to do."

Back at their camp, Jeff tied the horse, then stood looking at the other two. "I'm not sure this is over," he said. "I asked Pa if I could take you as far as you're going and see you get safe back home."

"Oh, Jeff." Leah reached out and took his arm. "Would you really do that?"

Jeff said, "Why, sure. What'd you think?"

"Come on, sit down," Leah said. "I've got a surprise for you."

The two boys sat, and Leah went back to her provision bag. "I baked these yesterday, so they're not fresh, but they're your favorite, Jeff."

Jeff looked at what she was holding out. "Fried pies! My land! I haven't had one of these in I don't know when." He grabbed one and sank his teeth into it. "Try one of these, Ezra," he said. "You ain't had no pie in your life until you've tasted one of Leah's fried pies."

Leah had learned to make fried pies from her mother. She simply cooked the dried fruit and wrapped it in dough and then dropped it into hot fat. They fried with a crispy brown exterior, and inside the fruit was juicy and tender.

The three consumed the six pies that she had brought, each eating two.

"I wish there was a hundred," Jeff declared, wiping his mouth with the back of his hand. "I could eat every one of them."

The fire crackled and hissed, and finally Jeff said, "I reckon we'll get an early start tomorrow." He looked then at the Yankee soldier. "Looks like you're gonna make it, Ezra."

"Well, I won't be fighting anymore. I promised Mr. Carter I wouldn't. So I'm out of it." He looked at Leah. "I'm glad of it too."

Jeff said, "I wish I was out of it. I wish all of us were."

From far off Leah heard the sound of a night bird making his last cries of the day, and then quiet settled down over the camp. They sat silently looking at the fire for a while, and she wondered what the future would bring.

After a while Leah said, "I guess we'd better get to bed."

They all got up then, and she went over to Jeff. "Good night, Jeff. And I can't thank you enough for what you've done." She turned and climbed into the wagon and rolled into her blankets.

"Guess we'll bunk out here," Jeff said. He took the blanket that Leah had given him, and Ezra did the same.

The two young men lay in the darkness, watching the moon. Then Ezra said, "Funny, isn't it—I

144

signed up to fight the Rebels, and here's one that saved my life. I sure do thank you."

"That's all right," Jeff said. He was already thinking of the time he would have to return to the fighting, and it depressed him. "Good night, Yank."

Ezra lifted himself up onto one elbow and smiled in the moonlight. "Good night, Johnny Reb," he said, then lay back and went to sleep.

17

Someday All This Will Be Over

Ezra sat in the rocking chair, holding the baby. He was singing to her a nursery song he had learned from Sarah Carter. There was a look on his face that Leah had never seen before.

"He sure is foolish about that baby, isn't he, Ma?"

In the next room, Mrs. Carter looked up from her sewing and smiled. "I never saw a young man take to a child so. Girls do sometimes. Sarah and I, of course, are silly about that child. But a young feller like Ezra—I never seen anything like that."

"I think it's because he didn't have any home life," Leah said. "He told me yesterday he'd never held a baby in his whole life. Isn't that terrible?"

"Well, as much as he loves Esther, I think he ought to have a dozen of his own. Unusual to see a young man like that."

She put her sewing into a basket and got up, pausing long enough to say, "You two have gotten to be pretty close, haven't you?"

"I guess so." Leah watched Ezra, who held the baby up now and squeezed her to make her chortle. "I felt so sorry for him when I first saw him, of course. He was about as sick as I ever saw anybody. Then after he got better, I got worried about him having to go back to that prison. I'm glad we were able to get him away."

She looked out the window to where Jeff was splitting wood. "I think it was noble of Jeff to do what he did. If he hadn't come for us, they would have caught us for sure."

"I wish Tom could have come back to see Sarah," her mother said.

"Does she say much about him, Ma?"

"No, she doesn't talk much. You know Sarah. She's just quiet. Half the young fellows in this neighborhood are trying to court her, but she just won't have anything to do with any of them."

"I think it's the same way with Tom. At least that's what Jeff says. It's a shame, isn't it, Ma? Two young people like that, wanting to get married and can't because of this old war."

Outside, Jeff was saying about the same thing to Leah's father.

Dan Carter was a thin man with brown hair and faded blue eyes. He was not in good health but had managed his job as a sutler better than anyone thought possible. Now he sat on an upturned box and watched Jeff split sections of beech.

Every time Jeff landed a blow, the wood fell as splintered as a cloven rock. "You're the best wood splitter I ever saw, Jeff," he said. "Don't waste your strength like so many fellers do." He watched the young man take aim, drive a hard blow, then reach down and pick up the wood and toss it onto a pile.

"Nothing hard about splitting wood." Jeff shrugged. "Kinda fun. I like it." He looked over then toward the house. "Not sure I did the right thing yet, Mr. Carter. Been worrying me some."

"You mean about helping an enemy soldier escape?"

"Yes, sir." Jeff frowned. "I know what would happen if I got caught doing it. I'd probably be shot or hanged. After all, he is the enemy."

"I suppose technically that's true, son," Mr. Carter said, "but somehow he just don't seem like he's much of a threat, does he? Never saw a quieter, meeker boy."

"Well, that's true enough. But some of these quiet ones, when the battle starts they turn into wildcats. I've seen it happen." He stacked an armload of wood and then said, "This ought to be enough to get you through a while. I'll cut some more before I leave."

They went back into the house, and Jeff dropped the wood into the woodbox. Then he turned to wash his hands at the sink.

"Why, Jeff," Leah's mother said, "you've cut enough wood to last for two weeks, I do believe. Why don't you rest a while?"

"I'm not gonna rest. I can do that when I get back. I'm gonna walk around and take a look at the country. I sure do miss it, Miz Carter."

"Well, why don't you and Leah go out and hunt birds' eggs? You haven't done that in a while."

Jeff laughed. "No, we haven't. Maybe we'll do that after lunch."

"It'll be ready soon. Don't go too far away."

Jeff walked into the living room and saw Ezra with the baby.

Ezra looked over and said, "This sister of yours, she's some girl, Jeff. Look at these dark eyes. I never seen such dark eyes."

Jeff grinned at Esther, who smiled at him and doubled up her fist and struck herself in the eye with it.

Both boys laughed, and Jeff said, "Yeah, she's growing up so fast, I can't believe it."

Leah joined them then. "Let me hold her a while. You haven't let her get out of your hands, Ezra."

Reluctantly Ezra surrendered the baby, and Leah kissed her on the cheek. "You're a precious thing," she whispered, "and going to be the prettiest girl in these mountains."

Ezra said quietly, "Well, maybe the second prettiest."

Leah's cheeks turned rosy.

Jeff gave the Union soldier a direct look but said nothing.

Later on they all sat down and ate the meal that Mrs. Carter and Sarah had prepared.

Sarah had dark hair and dark blue eyes, and Ezra had told Jeff, "I don't blame your brother for liking her. She sure is pretty."

Now, as they sat around the table, Mr. Carter said, "Well, we don't have all the family here, but we're grateful for what's here. Let's thank the Lord for the food."

They all bowed their heads.

He said a quick blessing and afterward smiled and said, "All right, pitch in. Your mother's a terrible cook, Leah, but no matter."

Mrs. Carter sniffed. "I notice you haven't turned anything down."

They ate heartily and then enjoyed some of the peach pie that Leah had baked.

Ezra said, "I'll sure miss this cooking when I'm gone, Mrs. Carter. I never ate such food in my life."

Dan Carter looked over at his wife.

Leah was watching, and she saw a look pass between them. She had often wondered how those two could understand each other without saying a word, but they did.

"Where are you going now, Ezra?"

Ezra shrugged his shoulders. "Don't rightly know, Mr. Carter. Not going to be in the army. I gave my parole to your brother, so I guess I'll go get a job somewhere."

Mary Carter looked at him over her coffee cup. "Don't you have any people at all, Ezra?"

"No, ma'am. Nobody. I guess I'll go back up North since it's the only place I know."

Dan said abruptly, "Why do you want to go up there? Do you like it up there, Ezra?"

"It's the only place I know," he repeated.

"I've been thinking," Mr. Carter said, "since I'm gone with the sutler business, this place sure needs a man's hand. We had a good helper, but he quit and went to the city. Why don't you just stay around here? Plenty of work for a young fellow like you."

Ezra stared at Dan Carter with a startled expression on his face. "Why, I never thought of it!" he exclaimed. His glance shifted at once to Leah, who smiled at him, then he nodded. "I can't think of anything in the world I'd rather do than work on a farm, specially with you folks. You wouldn't have to pay me—"

"Pay you! Why, of course, we'll pay you. The laborer is worthy of his hire." Dan slapped the table, making the dishes jingle.

"Now you stop that banging on the table," Mrs. Carter scolded her husband. Then she smiled at Ezra. "I don't know how good a hand you'd be in the field, but you're mighty good at taking care of younguns. You can give me and Sarah a rest now and then with Esther. You wouldn't mind that, would you?"

They all saw that young Ezra Payne was struggling with his feelings. He was staring down at his plate, and his fork was held so tightly in his right hand that his knuckles were white.

Silence fell over the table, and when Ezra looked up he had to blink. Finally, he muttered, "I'll do my best to please you."

After the meal was over, Jeff said, "Guess I'll go out and look things over."

"Take the gun along, Jeff," Mr. Carter said. "A rabbit or two would be pretty good in the pot."

"All right."

"I want to go too, Jeff," Leah said, "and I get to take a shot."

"Why, you couldn't hit a barn!"

"That's what you say. Come on, let's go."

As Leah and Jeff made their way down the road and disappeared into the woods, Ezra watched them. Then he said, "They're real good friends, aren't they, Miss Sarah?"

"Yes, they are. They've known each other all their lives. I think it broke Leah's heart when Jeff had to leave."

Ezra said nothing, but his eyes did not leave the place where the two had disappeared.

For Jeff, coming back to the old paths he had

walked so many times growing up was pure joy. He held the shotgun in the crook of his arm, his eyes going everywhere.

"Look," he said, "you remember the time Old Ranger and Pink treed the bobcat over there in that big sycamore? We tried to knock him out with rocks. Remember that?"

Leah laughed. "Weren't we birds, though? If that cat had come down, I bet you would have seen a pair of scared kids taking off."

Jeff grinned. "We really got into some pickles. It's a wonder your folks—or mine—didn't wear out a peach tree switch on both of us."

"They did once or twice."

"Yes, they did," he agreed.

As they crested a rise, he looked down on the valley and said, "I don't want to go see our home place. It'd just remind me of what things used to be like."

They walked for an hour and shot two rabbits. Jeff expressed amazement that Leah actually hit one. "First time you ever hit anything," he teased. He put the rabbits in a sack and carried them. "Here, you carry the gun."

They finally came to the creek and made their way down to the bridge.

"Don't have time to go trying to catch Old Napoleon"—the huge bass that inhabited that part of the river. Jeff had caught him once and let him go. "I hate to go back," he said suddenly.

"Someday, Jeff, all this war will be over."

Jeff turned to Leah, noticing the brightness of her eyes. She was wearing a simple green dress that matched her eyes, and the breeze was causing her hair to blow. Somehow he'd never noticed before how smooth her cheeks were and how clean her jawline was. Suddenly he said, "I never thought about Ezra staying here."

"I'm glad he is, though. He doesn't have anywhere else to go, and he likes my family."

"He likes *you*," Jeff said, his jaw growing tight.

Leah stared at him. "Why, Jeff! I think you're jealous."

"Jealous? Who's jealous?"

"You are! I can tell." She laughed at him and said, "You don't have any business being jealous. After all, you went absolutely cockeyed every time Lucy Driscoll walked by. I never saw a boy behave so foolishly."

Jeff glared, and his face reddened, perhaps because he knew she spoke the truth. "I don't want to talk about that," he snapped.

He turned and walked quickly off, and Leah ran to catch up with him. "Jeff," she said, "don't be mad."

He abruptly stopped and faced her. "I'm sorry, Leah. Don't know what's the matter with me. It's all right if you like Ezra."

Leah smiled suddenly. "I'm glad for your permission. It's all right if you like Lucy too, if you want to."

"I don't want to. I stopped liking her the minute she said she looked at that letter. That wasn't right."

They stood there for a long time until finally he said, "Leah . . ."

"Yes, Jeff?"

He shifted uncomfortably. "It's all right if you like Ezra better than you like me."

Leah put her hand on his cheek. She leaned forward and whispered, "He's real nice, but he's not my best friend, Jeff."

He was silent. Then he reached up and covered her hand with his own and smiled. He said quietly, "Come on, we'd better go back."

They turned and walked back down the path, Leah's hand secure in Jeff's. She looked up at him, and the world suddenly seemed not so dark.

The sun was shining, the birds were singing, and she whispered, "Some day, Jeff, we'll come back to all this."